WITHDRAWN FROM
CIRCULATION

D0962070

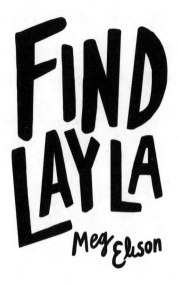

FIND LAYLA

Meg Elison

ALSO BY MEG ELISON

The Road to Nowhere Series

The Book of the Unnamed Midwife
The Book of Etta
The Book of Flora

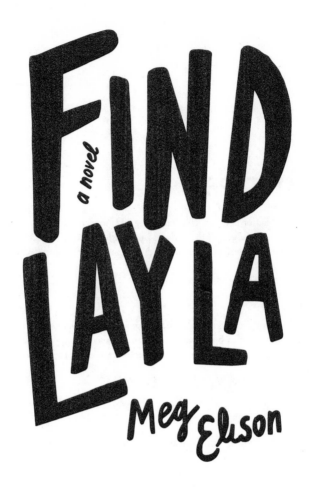

FIND
LAYLA

a novel

Meg Elison

█▙▟█ SKYSCAPE

▌▌▌ SKYSCAPE

Text copyright © 2020 by Meg Elison
All rights reserved.

Published by Skyscape, New York

www.apub.com

Amazon, the Amazon logo, and Skyscape are trademarks of Amazon.com, Inc., or its affiliates.

ISBN-13: 9781542019804 (hardcover)
ISBN-10: 154201980X (hardcover)

ISBN-13: 9781542019781 (paperback)
ISBN-10: 1542019788 (paperback)

Cover design by Kimberly Glyder

Printed in the United States of America

First edition

*For Beau, who made the bread-crumb trail with me
and followed it to the other side of the woods.*

*And for Maggie, who knew the way out and held my
hand until we found it.*

I did my first science experiment in the bathtub with dish soap and a knife. That bath seems like the place to start, because it was my first laboratory and my first failure. It happened a long time ago, before my brother was born. It feels like it happened to somebody else—to a little girl who wanted to be a scientist but didn't really know anything.

She got the idea from watching a shampoo commercial. Commercials always looked the same—a woman went into the shower and filled her hair with bubbling suds. She scrubbed and smiled and rinsed, and then her hair fell down shiny and heavy and perfect for the camera. The little girl figured she could replicate those results, so she grabbed her supplies and headed for the bathtub.

She filled the tub halfway and got in. For months, she had been pulling her hair back in a ponytail-loop thing to hide the fact that it was all locked into three big knots. Well, today was the day they would be gone. She didn't know that those knots were a biome for spores and bacteria. She didn't know what the reaction would be when she intro-duced a lysis agent. She didn't know anything, not even how to brush her own hair.

Sitting in the hot water, the little girl poured out a handful of bright-yellow lemon-smelling dish soap and clapped it right to her wet head. The commercial said the soap would break up grease, and her hair felt greasy. It was a primitive hypothesis, and she had an idea for a test. She poured out a second handful and did it again, on the other side. She set the bottle down and started to work it in.

Her head foamed up and the suds started to drip over her eyebrows. She thought about the woman in the commercial and she scrubbed and smiled, scrubbed and smiled. The bubbles ran into her eyes. They stung and watered, but she didn't want to be a baby and cry about it. She worked it all the way through and then lay back in the water to rinse it out.

Her hair didn't fall down shiny and heavy and perfect for the camera. The soap stripped all the dirt and oil out of it; the bathwater turned gray under the layer of gasoline-rainbow soap bubbles. The lysis reaction was successful. Her curly mess of hair was now dry as a broomstick and locked tighter than ever, but at least it was clean. She was a pretty stupid little girl, and she'd been expecting this to work better. The experiment did not produce the anticipated results, but she didn't call it a failure. She observed that the process was difficult and would be hard to replicate.

She picked up the knife next.

It was a heavy-handled kitchen knife, actually meant for cutting the bones out of pieces of meat. It was sharp, and she at least knew enough to point it away from herself. Holding her first fat knot at the ends, she took a deep breath, closed her eyes tight, and stabbed into the middle, pulling downward to cut it into smaller knots. She did it again and again, trying to get closer to her scalp.

This wasn't science. This part was just work. The first knot was exhausting. She had cut it into six finger-size pieces, and her arms ached from holding them up and working through each chunk. Her eyes stung. The knife ripped through her hair with a sound like sawing meat. She didn't care; she got through the first and started on the next one. When she had sliced up her knots as much as she dared, and managed somehow not to cut herself, she put the knife down and got the brush.

She tried to start at the top of her head and brush down, but even she could see that would never work. She switched and started at the bottom, pulling out an inch at a time, working up to the scalp. Most of what was detangled from the locks fell out and caught in the bristles of the brush. Some of it went into the tub. A little bit stayed on her head. After a few locks, she had to yank out a small rug of hair from the brush so that it would keep working. These she laid on the floor beside the tub. They piled up wet and straggly, like something a cat would leave behind.

The little girl wanted to stop. Her arms were tired. Her bathwater was cold. Her head and neck hurt all over. She did cry like a little baby, because it was all so *hard*. I wish I could tell her that's life.

Life is hard and complicated and messy. Life is parasites that live in your gut and brilliant scientists teaching a gorilla to use sign language. Life is moths that drink tears, and the flu virus, and nothing you can control. Life is sometimes using a knife to comb your hair, because absolutely nothing else works, and life always finds a way through. I want to tell her what I always tell myself now: that's life. It cheers me up and it calms me down. It reminds me to focus on what I can do rather than what I can't.

That's life. Even back then, she understood. She kept up the hard and painful work, and she got through it. After what seemed like forever, she had some awful, ragged, chopped-up curls still attached to her head. She could pull her brush all the way through it. It squeaked when she touched it, and it looked like the coat of a shelter dog. She didn't care. That was a successful experiment.

That little moron sat there with her red eyes and her cold dirty bathwater, brushing her hair slowly, glancing bristles off her aching scalp, thinking that her hair was as soft and clean as the hair of a princess.

I guess I can let her have a moment. But really, what an idiot.

She's me. I did that. I'm not pretending she's not me. It's just that a lot has happened since then.

3

That time I experimented on my own hair with a knife and dish soap in the bathtub wasn't the first time I knew there was something wrong with my mom. Or wrong with me. That we were doing it wrong. But it was the first time I realized that help was not on the way. It was the first time I went from being a subject to being an observer—to really doing science.

It was the first time I just took care of it myself.

Hard to pick a place to begin, but I believe that's how all this got started. You probably want to know about my video, everybody asks me about that. Some people ask me about #FindLayla and if I got anything out of it. People ask me where my brother is now.

I stand by that video and everything that came after.

What I got out of it . . . that's complicated.

And my brother is gone.

Monday 6:45 a.m.

Every day I hope that the walk to school will air out my clothes enough so that they can't smell it.

I walk slowly, leaving early. I read a book while I'm walking. I used to bump into stuff and worry about the crosswalks, but I've got it down these days. My little brother starts an hour later, so I get to walk alone. I used to take the straight route along the street, passing the pizza place and the magic shop that hustles me out when I go in to just look. After we moved to this town and got settled, I found the back way that took me through the park. There's a tiny break in the wall that's overgrown on both sides with honeysuckle. You can barely tell it's there, but I found it.

I looked up the flowers before I touched them. They're Caprifoliaceae. Common here in Southern California. Not poison. Good for bees. I drink from the little yellow trumpets sometimes, pulling them off the vine and biting through the green cup at the bottom of the gold. They're full of sweet nectar that tastes a little like their perfume smells. I tried rubbing it on myself once, but I just got sticky.

Fourteen is too old to be sticky.

I'll have to walk home with Kristi, who lives about eight blocks away, and my little brother. He always comes home with me. Kristi

Sanderson is my best friend. She's a lot sometimes, but she always loans me her phone or her laptop. She takes my side when other kids pick on me. Mostly. She reads me her poetry and shows me her drawings. What we have is symbiosis: that relationship between two organisms where they both get something they need out of it, like clown fish and anemones have. Like the anemone, she's got secret sharp places. Like the clown fish, I've got better defenses than most of my kind. It works.

Today I like the walk, because the fog rolled in over the park. The weather guy on the news calls it the marine layer. I watch the weather guy (because my phone is garbage) long enough to find out if I need to wear my old shoes in the rain and then change at school into my better ones. My socks stay wet all day, but at least nobody knows.

Then I switch to the channel that plays *The X-Files* from five to seven a.m. I like to watch Dr. Scully work to explain the impossible but always return to what she knows she can prove. It's an old show, but it's really cool. And there aren't that many women scientists on TV nowadays.

If I get to school early enough, there's free breakfast for anybody who gets free lunch. They butter the toast before they put it in the oven, so it comes out hot and golden and bubbly on top. It's stupid how much I look forward to this.

In the cafeteria, the floor is wet and my shoes slip a little. The bottom of the left one is mostly duct tape. It doesn't stop the leak, *and* it's slippery. Failed experiment, but I don't have another hypothesis. I manage to stay upright and head into the tunnel where we get our plates. A couple of girls on shift this week are people I know; when the breakfast program started, they also started a work program so we could see what life is gonna be like. On one hand, life is bound to suck and involve a drive-thru window. On the other hand, you get to eat as much leftover breakfast as you want after your shift. I'm not on for a few more days.

They load me up with the fakest eggs in existence, a fruit cup, and my favorite thing in the world: magical buttery whole-wheat toast triangles. The toast stays soft in the middle, a perfect golden circle where the butter sinks into the bread while it pools in the heat of the oven. I munch around it in a circle, eating the dark-brown crusts and saving the best bite for last.

I sit on one of the long benches that folds out of the wall and reopen my book. Breakfast is not even half as loud as lunch, and people are too zombie-eyed to make fun of me. Mornings are just better.

The girls across the table are loudly advertising their ignorance, and it's hard work to tune them out. I resort to pretending to read while eating and try to keep my eye rolling to a minimum. Wish I had big headphones.

"Yeah but I heard if you shave your junk, your hair comes back darker."

"That's seriously true. After I started shaving, it's all dark and way thicker than before."

"That doesn't make any sense. When you cut your hair it doesn't grow in darker than before."

One of them is nodding her head with her mouth open, an expression that makes me want to punch people. I look back down at my book.

"Yeh-huh. I had blonde hair as a baby, and now it's all brown. It's because they cut it. If they left it alone, I'd still be blonde, plus it'd be way long. Plus, you never see pubes in pics. You gotta do it, but once you start you can't stop."

They Google it, then argue with Google. I wish there was Wi-Fi on campus so I could live-tweet this conversation. For once, I'd be the one sharing someone else's embarrassing moments. But I can't connect, and if I write it down and tweet it from a computer later it won't be as good.

They finally get up and leave, not bothering to clear their trays. I don't move until they're through the cafeteria doors.

After they're gone, I swipe their toast.

1:45 p.m.

"I don't understand why I can't stay over. You've been to my house a thousand times. I've never even met your mom. Just your dumb-ass stink-bomb brother."

Kristi is making that face in the mirror again. The one that makes her lips look bigger and her cheeks look smaller. She'll do it for a few minutes and then finally take a picture.

I've seen it enough times to know that I don't care and that it doesn't matter what I think. She'll keep the pic or delete it no matter what I say, based on whether she thinks she looks fat or her freckles are too clear to get filtered out.

But the real problem here is that she said Andy was stinky. He totally is, but I need to know what kind of stink she meant. Is it his little-boy-won't-bathe stink, or something else? We live in the same house, in the same room, usually in the same bed, because he has nightmares and I can't tell him no. Maybe the morning walk isn't working.

I've waited too long to answer.

"We're not even real friends. If we were, you'd want me to come over and see your room. We could stay up watching those old movies you love. The ones you're always trying to tell me about."

She means the ones she always thinks are lame and makes fun of. Yes, that sounds great.

"Kristi, I'm sorry. My mom doesn't let me have people over. She just . . . hates it. I don't know why, okay?"

She makes the face again and takes a pic. The flash lights up the room and makes her a white redheaded nobody. My eyes get that green burned spot for a minute, and I blink. In the long, echoing girls' bathroom, I'm nobody, too. Hair pulled back tight. No makeup. I tell people I'm allergic, because it's easier than admitting I don't have any and don't know how to use it. Lipstick kisses smear all along the chipped bottom of the mirror, but not one from me. I'd love to grow a culture from the edge of that mirror and show them what they're really kissing. If we had some agar plates, I could do it. But we haven't gotten to that experiment yet in class.

If Kristi will let me borrow her phone, I can sign into my Instagram and post a photo explaining the experiment, since I can't really do it. But now does not seem like a good time to ask.

"Shit. No, it's not okay." She turns off her flash and does the face again. I know she'll hate her forehead wrinkles, but I don't say anything. "That's not fair. It's your house, too. Why is she like that? Can your brother's friends come over?"

Shutter noise, another delete.

"No, nobody can."

"What about your mom's friends?"

I have never met anyone who was my mom's friend. I consider the possibility that she has some, somewhere.

"Nope, not even them."

"That's fucked up."

"Sorry."

She finally gets a picture she can use, so we leave the bathroom. The breezeway is deserted.

"Shit. We're late."

I still don't take off.

"I didn't hear the late bell." Kristi pulls her backpack up to her shoulders and shrugs into it. "Okay, see you later."

She runs away at that, her backpack bouncing on her like it's totally empty. I turn and walk the other way. My class is way out in the trailers.

I miss the late bell; Kristi texts later that she doesn't. That's life.

3:45 p.m.

"I want to go to the pool!" He's whining again. He's always whining when he wants something.

"Well, I don't want to go to the pool. And since you can't go without someone to watch you, looks like you're not going."

Kristi is walking a little ahead of us. She drifts off anytime Andy talks.

"Once this once!"

"What?" I look down at him and see that he's trying very hard to win me over. The juice-box stains around his mouth make him look like a baby. He stops scowling.

"Once this once. Once this once."

His lisp makes this sentence even worse than it should be. *Yes, repeating it helps a lot. Great.* Kids are so stupid that I don't know why anyone has them.

"I think you mean 'Just this once.' And the answer is still no. Because I take you all the time, so it isn't once. Could you not bother me to death, please?"

He's only six. I hate disappointing him. I know he'll be bored at home, but I can't spend another night dragging him out of the pool after dark while he screams at me.

Last time, I couldn't get him to leave until after nine. The water was warm and the night air was cold. No towels. No reason to go home. Finally I just walked out, shivering, by myself and told him I was leaving without him. He caught up to me a few minutes later, crying.

The scowl is back. "You're mean. You're mean and you don't care about anybody but yourself!"

"Okay, whatever, Andy." I jog a little and catch up to Kristi.

"So, what are you doing tonight?" She's doing that thing where she's listening to me talk but staring at her phone. I never know if she's hearing me or not.

"I don't know. My stepdad is gonna be home, so I'll probably hide out in my room. Since I don't have anywhere else to go." She looks away from her phone just enough to show me her face arranged along

beautifully sad lines, tragic like an Insta model who's lost her sponsor-
ship. Then she goes back to it, her face blank.

I don't say anything. My solid strategy.

"What are you gonna do?"

"Homework," I lie. All my homework is done, and she's gone.

Andy catches up, and we go through the iron gate to our apartment
complex. Once upon a time we shared a key to get in, but the lock
broke more than a year ago. The hinges screech and the springs slam
the gate shut behind us. We walk around the stucco corner, trotting a
little faster with home coming into view. Andy goes up the stairs first, as
always. We've figured out how to do this fast and never be seen. He gets
to the top and looks around while I come up behind. The coast is clear.

He climbs on the black banister and leans out over the gap between
the stairs and the building. It's about a foot wide, and the drop is two
stories. I don't think either of us can slip through, but the fear is real every
time. Andy tugs at the window and it slides over, knocking the blinds
around. He shoves his backpack through, and we hear it hit the floor.
Then he lifts one knee up onto the air conditioner just below the window.
I boost him up the last foot and a half, and he goes through the blinds
into the dark.

I toss my backpack in after him and look over my shoulder again.
Still clear. I push up on the banister and lay my belly across the AC unit.
I pull with both hands to slide over the windowsill, which hurts from
the band of my training bra down to my knees, and slip headfirst to the
floor. I stand up, blinking until my eyes adjust, and close the window.
I wait until the blinds stop swinging and then go to find the hurricane
lantern. It's a tall glass old-school lamp that works through the surface
tension of its fuel and the capillary action of its wick. It's kind of cool,
but I wish I didn't need it.

It doesn't slosh when I shake it. Out of lamp oil.

I feel around to find the candle I left in the kitchen. I turn on the
stove to light it, but nothing happens.

Sighing, I make my way carefully to the couch. Somewhere at the edge of the dining room my foot slides into something mushy and slimy, like a banana a few days past ripe. I ignore it. I push my hands deep into the couch cushions and reject stale crackers and empty cigarette packs until I find what I was looking for.

One plastic BIC lighter. I push down the little button with my thumb, and it's the kind that flares straight up like a jet engine. I take it to the candle and light it, light all the ones I can find. I light the lamp after all, figuring that the wick is soaked enough to burn for at least a little while. I'm right.

Andy has a Fruit Roll-Up crammed in his teeth. I wonder what else is in the kitchen. "I want to watch TV."

"Yeah, well. Good luck with that."

He sulks, kicking something unseen. "Wanted to sing the pineapple song."

I wait until he's distracted and quiet enough to tiptoe away.

I go to our bedroom, headed straight for my secret hideout. A milk crate beneath the window, the glass covered with foil. The window open just enough. Hours of quiet on the other side. If he's bored enough, he'll find me. He might come looking for me any minute. I'm running out of time already. I need him distracted, and without the TV he won't be.

Screw it.

I turn my back on my spot and find him trying to pull a couple of tightly joined Legos apart. That might have kept him busy awhile, but the light is fading. Once he can't see, it's all over. Can't do anything then but go to bed, and he's not tired. I'm not tired. Well, not sleepy. We've got to do something else.

"Come on, Andy. Let's just go to the pool."

He jumps to get his trunks. I undress and pull on my blue thrift-store bathing suit, still wet from yesterday and cold enough to make me break out in gooseflesh all over.

We walk to the apartment-complex pool and get dinner from the vending machine there. We count our change and pick one short can of Pringles and one big bag of Twizzlers. We swim for hours, the pool water warm and cloudy, with pennies and secret surprise broken glass at the bottom. There's a little bit of Wi-Fi signal at the pool, so I tweet that I'm going night swimming. That sounds like something a normal kid would do, right? I leave my phone on a chair and swim with Andy, keeping him away from the deep end. We talk about how cool it is now that the gate that's supposed to keep the pool safe is broken and we can just step on the bottom rung to open it. We argue over who can hold their breath the longest and how fun it is to float on our backs. Nobody else is in the pool tonight, so it's just us. Still, we're careful.

We don't talk about our dark house where the lights don't work and the gas is definitely off again. We don't talk about how long it's been since the front door stopped opening, or how scared we are of the window climb every day. He doesn't ask me when Mom will be home, which is great because I have no idea.

9:45 p.m.

It isn't as much of a fight to get him out this time. I climb up the pool ladder and hug myself in the cold and tell him it's time. He comes up after a minute or two, hugging himself the same way. We can't see our breath, but our fingers are prunes, and his hair hangs pointy in his face like icicles. We don't have towels. We walk home like penguins, arms and legs tight together and straight, our backs to the wind.

I boost him through the window and then come up slowly, extra careful because I'm soaking wet and I have imagined myself falling like a thousand times. I don't fall, but the corner of the AC unit leaves a long, angry scratch down my bare thigh. I look at the beads of blood welling up, wondering if the chlorine on my skin is enough to disinfect. Blood, bacteria, uncertainty. That's life.

I only light one candle this time. We drop our wet suits on the floor and scavenge something to sleep in. I come up with a big shirt covered in soda logos; he finds a pair of underwear or shorts. It's impossible to tell which and hard to care.

We slowly climb up the ladder to my loft bed, each of us using one hand. I have the candle, he has a book. He reads aloud to me like we do every night, and I trace the pattern of spaceships on the mattress, thinking about adventures somewhere else. We each huddle under our own blanket, and he laughs at the funny parts of his book. He still doesn't ask when she'll be home.

I guess he doesn't care anymore, either.

Tuesday 2:56 a.m.

I think that was her. I hold my breath for a minute. The candle's out, and Andy didn't wake up. I hear the snick of the lighter, smell the smoke a minute later.

Mom's home.

Tuesday 11:36 a.m.

Everybody's phone is better than mine.

On my right, the new iPhone. Tall, skinny, stylish. Just like the guy who holds it. He's scrolling through girls' profiles. I recognize some of them.

On my left, a new Android. Shiny and bright, and the girl holding it doesn't even bother to try to hide it. Phones out all over the room. No one cares.

In the front of the room, Mr. Raleigh. He's lecturing on monocots or eudicots or dicots right now. Pictures of leaves on the big screen. I haven't been keeping up, but I know when he's checking the cracked screen of his old iPhone, because he looks down at his lap behind his desk and frowns or smiles.

In my pocket, a no-name knockoff phone that hasn't had minutes on it since summer vacation. It only works when I have Wi-Fi, and I guess the school knows we'd never quit texting or watching YouTube if they offered it. I still plug it in at night so that I can take pictures with the squinty little camera and keep time. I take it out and pretend to text on it when I need a minute to myself. I have a set of funny and mean things to say when people ask for my number. It never rings.

Pistil, stamen, sepal. I open my gallery and scroll through the pictures I took last week. Kristi and me eating french fries at the Jack in the Box by the high school. She passes for a high-school girl, and even though I'm a year older than she is, I don't. That's life.

A blurry close-up of a honeysuckle, another of a rose. The flowers remind me to look up occasionally and check in with Mr. Raleigh. This time it's a good thing, because he's staring at me.

"Layla?"

Not a chance that I'll guess correctly.

"I'm sorry, what was the question?" I close my phone with one hand and move it slowly toward my pocket.

Raleigh sighs. "What is the circled structure on the slide called?"

I looked up for a second. The little green cup under a flower. I look back at him.

"Calyx."

"Yes. Thank you. Try to stay with us."

My face burns. On my right, the iPhone disappears. On my left, the Android doesn't even waver.

I stay after class. Raleigh is a nice guy and I feel bad.

"I'm sorry I've been so out of it, Mr. Raleigh. I'm doing the reading and the homework. I'm just daydreamy in class."

He's smiling at his lap.

"Okay, I'll see you later," I tell him, already sliding toward the door.

As I turn to leave, he clues in. "Hey, Layla. Come on back. Sorry, I just had to check something. So, what's up with you? Why were you absent two days last week? Are you okay?"

He's got that look of polite concern. I'd know it anywhere; it means a grown-up is worried but can't actually do anything to help.

"Yeah, I'm fine. I was just sick last week. I aced the Friday test anyway, so it doesn't really matter."

"No, I guess it doesn't. Still, you don't seem . . ."

Oh god please stop looking at me. Please don't notice that I've taped my shoes together or that my jeans haven't been washed in a month. Please tell me this flannel makes me look grunge on purpose rather than gross on accident. Please just don't even look at my hair.

I stare at the floor.

"Is everything okay?" His voice is too kind, too soft.

This response is ready, has always been ready without question or any time to think.

"Yeah, everything's fine."

He's trying to catch my eye, but I can't look.

"You know, I've never even met your mother," Raleigh says. "She's never come to a parent-teacher conference. She signed the paperwork to get you into the honors program, but other than that, I've never even gotten an email."

She signed that paperwork the same way she's signed everything for Andy and me since she registered him for kindergarten: in my handwriting. Am I supposed to be emailing my teachers as her? Do the other parents do that? What do they ask?

"She just works all the time, Mr. Raleigh. She's not into all this."

He tilts his head to the side, at an angle that makes his huge nose look even bigger. Black eyes on mine, and that look of concern is back, but pity is creeping in. If I could shoot ink out of my butt and swim away like a squid, I would.

"Okay. Just let me know if there's anything I can—" There's a faraway buzzing sound, and he's frowning at his crotch again.

"Anything you say, Mr. Raleigh." And I can finally escape.

Lunch

Kristi's lunch kills me. It kills me every day, so I've died hungry at least a thousand times.

Her mom packs it for her, and it looks like something out of a magazine ad, like no real food ever looks. Today it's a bento with brown rice and a line of shrimp, all pink and perfect. Seaweed salad in one of the small compartments and orange slices in the other. She also has a pack of kale chips, but they don't fit in the box.

Kristi will eat one, maybe two bites of her shrimp and rice before turning the box upside down over a trash can. She'll ignore the seaweed salad because it gets caught in her braces, and into the garbage it will go. She'll eat all the kale chips right now, saying that they're the only thing she likes.

"These chips are the only thing that bitch packs me that I even like." Crunch crunch crunch.

School lunch today is spaghetti with the cheese on top that looks like dandruff. Canned peaches on the side and a carton of milk. Every day, I try to figure out how to eat it slowly while looking disinterested. Watching Kristi whack her lunch box against the side of the garbage can to throw away her pretty food, I know that today I will fail.

"Do you think Emerson likes me?" She's looking across the room at Emerson Berkeley, the semigoth hotness in our class. He's reading, as usual.

"Maybe. That one time in geometry, he thought your cartoon was really funny." I eat more spaghetti, thinking of her seaweed salad. The dressing on it is black and full of sesame seeds. I bet it's good.

Kristi makes a face. "That was like a year ago. I don't even draw cartoons anymore."

"Yeah, but you should." I'm staring at Emerson now, his black leather and black skin and black hair and black eyeliner. He looks like a rock star who adopts three-legged dogs.

"What?"

My eyes snap back to Kristi and I can see she's pissed at me. No idea why.

"Your cartoons. You should go back to them. They were really good, remember how Emerson said—"

She's red in the face, blood-pink under her red-orange hair. Oh god, here it comes.

"You know that I stopped drawing my comics when my dad moved out! I told you I'd never draw again after Sean moved in! Those comics were about my family and now my family is *gone!*" Tears come up in her red-rimmed green eyes but don't spill.

Kristi's temper is like a lion (*Panthera leo leo*, king of the loud but lazy). It needs to roar a lot and get noticed, but it's not really gonna do anything. It'll wait for someone else to do the work.

"I'm sorry, Kris. I didn't mean to . . . I was just thinking of proof that Emerson likes you. That's all. And I'm sure he does."

Now she has to choose. Be the lioness and change the subject to boys that like her (her favorite subject) or keep throwing her endless fit about her parents' divorce. I watch her while she tries to decide.

Her little pink compact mirror comes out, and she blots under her eyes. "I think he does like me. I think you're right. Even if you had to say it in such an insensitive way." She runs a brown pencil under her eyes again, fixing herself up and going back to staring at the daydream-dressed-like-a-nightmare boy. Emerson gets up to leave, and she's bored again.

My lunch tray is empty. I resist the desire to run a finger through the biggest rectangle, to pick up the last whisper of red sauce and lick it.

"I guess you wouldn't know what it's like," she says in a whiny little voice.

"What?" I look at the empty spot where Emerson used to be. If she thinks I don't know what it's like to have a crush on the boy everyone has a crush on, she's a crappy best friend.

"My life. You don't know what it's like to go through a divorce. How it wrecks your life. What it's like to only see your dad on the weekends, and live with some asshole your mom married. You don't get how hard it is, that's why you don't care about my feelings."

"I said I was sorry," I tell her, trying to sound sympathetic.

She's looking in the mirror again. "Nobody understands. Not even my best friend."

She's right. I don't.

5:40 p.m.

Sometimes I think Kristi invites me over just so that she can have an audience for her suffering.

She plugs her phone into her speakers, puts on some emo band, and tells me to sit down on her bed. Her bed is all pale pink. It has a canopy above it with tiny glow-in-the-dark stars her mom put in it, so that when we lie on our backs in the dark it's like we're in a safe, enclosed universe of soft pink skies.

The whole house smells like cinnamon pancakes.

Kristi changes into a long black skirt and a black leather jacket that looks way too big for her.

"Okay, listen to this:

Son of no sun
beach in the rain
you're an enigma
with an old poet's name."

She switches back from her poetry voice into her normal voice. "Get it? Because his name is Emerson, like that one guy?"

"Yeah, I get it. That's clever."

"Thanks!" She smiles wide, but then gets her serious pout back on. She lifts her black leather arms and sways just a little.

"Wild dark angel
with raven's wings
you shine like a dark star
among the dull things."

"You use the word *dark* twice."

She frowns and looks back at the piece of paper on her pale-pink desk.

Kristi's mom, Bette, knocks at the door. She talks to us without opening it.

"Hey, sweetie, will you two be ready for dinner in about thirty minutes?"

"Yeah, Mom." Kristi's getting out another sheet of her pretty paper.

"Okay, see you downstairs, then."

While Kristi's back is turned to me, I look around her room. Her shoe collection is mixed up all over the bottom of her closet, but her clothes are hung straight. It looks like she has about forty pairs of jeans. She tapes posters up all over the walls with that special blue tape that won't mess up the pale-pink paint. I try to imagine what this room would look like if it was mine. What if Bette was my mom and the room was pale green and that was my MacBook just casually lying on the floor?

No, I'd never leave it on the floor. Not if I had my own pale-green desk.

"Hey, Kristi?"

She doesn't look back at me. "What?"

"Hey, is it cool if I do it now? Your mom said we have like half an hour, and you're pretty involved in your poem. So, cool?"

"Yeah, sure. My stuff is in the bottom drawer, help yourself." She's distracted.

I'm out the door as she asks, "What's another word for *dark*?"

"Benighted," I answer, not even slowing down.

Kristi hates her bathroom because she has to share it. Her mom and stepdad have one in their bedroom, and there's one for guests downstairs. That leaves this one to Kristi and her older sister, Karly. Karly goes to Stanford, so really Kristi hardly shares it at all.

I told Kristi that I wanted to try shaving my legs for the first time, but that my mom wouldn't let me do it at home. She loved the idea of me shaving my "gorilla legs," as she called them, and told me to come over for dinner.

In the bottom drawer I find her pink razors and shaving cream, lost in a bunch of other junk. I turn to the deep white bathtub and mess with the knobs until hot water comes out. I pull up the lever to block the drain and strip off my clothes. When I climb in, the water burns my toes and I have to hop back out. More messing with the knobs and frantically kicking at the water until it drops to a temperature I can deal with.

Watching the clock, I wash my hair quickly and comb some of Kristi's conditioner through it, leaving the slick stuff in for a while. I pull one leg out of the water and smear shaving cream all over it. How hard can this be?

I drag the razor down from my ankle, like I've seen people do in commercials. The tricky part is how much pressure to use. I think I'm getting the hang of it when Bette walks in on me.

"Oh! Sorry, Layla. I didn't know you were in here. I was just looking for dirty laundry."

She bends down to pick up my clothes.

"Wait, no. Those are mine, I need those."

She's looking at the handful of jeans and underwear she snatched up off the tile, and then she looks at me.

"Why don't you let me throw these in the washer for you, honey?" There's that too-kind voice again.

I'm holding my folded arms against my chest and I want her out of here, but it's her house. I want her to put my clothes back down, but it'd actually be great if she washed them. I just don't have anything else to wear in the meantime.

With the exact same look of concern Mr. Raleigh showed me, she's staring at me now. "I can bring you something of mine to wear to dinner, and these won't take long."

I don't say anything. I don't know how.

She leans down and picks up my T-shirt and my shredded two-year-old training bra, too.

"Layla . . . there are some things your mom might not have told you. About hygiene."

How hard is it to drown yourself in the bathtub?

Her face says she knows we just hit maximum awkward. "I just want you to know that you can talk to me about anything." She's turning to leave. I study my leg as she walks out the door.

My ankle drips blood into the water.

At dinner I'm wearing her yellow tracksuit. Kristi laughs a little but doesn't even ask. She's happy that her stepdad is working late. She picks at dinner and drinks coffee just to make her mom mad. Coffee is my favorite, but I don't drink it at Bette's house. I know it makes her unhappy.

Kristi doesn't ask me how my first shave went.

8:00 p.m.

After two more readings of Kristi's poem and some ice cream, I'm walking home in clean clothes. It feels strange but nice.

I climb over the AC and through the window, and the lights are on inside. Mom's on the couch, a wreath of smoke around her. Andy's on the floor, surrounded by balled-up taco wrappers. The TV is jabbering.

"Mom got us some tacos, but you weren't here, so I eated them all," Andy says.

"That's okay that you *ate* them all. I ate at Kristi's."

Mom talks without looking at me. "I got a call at the office today from the school. Again. You let him go in dirty clothes. Again. I need some help around here."

"I need quarters to do the laundry, Mom."

She doesn't say anything, but I know that tomorrow or the next day two rolls of quarters will show up somewhere that I'll see them.

I walk past Andy toward our bedroom. As soon as I get into the hallway, my toes go squish and I know the bathroom's flooding again. With a sigh, I push the door open.

I think the sink got clogged three months ago, that's how it started. Mom used a wrench and pulled the pipe bend out from under the sink, but a piece broke and she couldn't put it back. So she put a big white bucket underneath it, because that faucet runs constantly and the water has to go somewhere. Mom realized after a few days that the bucket would fill up unless somebody was there to empty it all the time, but by the end of the day it was too heavy to lift. So she brought home a hacked-up length of garden hose. So now, once or twice a day, some-body has to suck the end of the hose and get the water flowing, then drop the end into the bathtub so it can drain.

When I say "somebody," I mean me. Andy can't remember to do it. And Mom can't handle anything.

This is called *siphoning*, and I learned how to do it years ago, when Mom taught me how to steal gas out of someone else's car. I put my mouth to the hose and breathe in the smell of mold. I pretend I don't, and I suck until I can feel the water coming. Not fast enough, though, and I get a mouthful of cold bucket water before I can stop it. I spit the water into the tub and let the bucket drain.

Nobody really knows how a siphon works. It's an incredibly com-plicated process involving gravity, tension, cohesion, and friction. A scientist named Bernoulli kind of explained it once, but it's mostly a mystery. I think I understand it better than most.

Next to the front door there's a stack of newspapers that's almost as tall as me. Mom brings home more every couple of days. I don't know where she got the idea, but it's been going on so long that I'm used to it now. Like climbing through the window. I head over to the stack and pick up an armload. I drop them on the floor as I go, spreading fresh paper out all over the wet hallway, on top of the last layer of newspaper.

It's about six inches deep now. Newspaper that takes on water swells up and sweats ink as it slowly breaks down. When I walk through the house barefoot, it splashes cold and black up my ankles with a gross squishing sound. For a few minutes after I put down fresh papers, the floor is dry and fairly firm. Don't look or smell and it's almost nice.

I get into bed and fold my clean clothes up and lay them in the corner to wear tomorrow. Andy crawls in hours later, smelling like tacos. I turn to face the wall.

Wednesday 6:30 a.m.

The quarters are sitting on top of the TV. Mom's gone.

Andy leaves for school after I've started the first load. The laundry room isn't technically open, but Mom gave me keys to all of the laundry rooms in the complex a long time ago.

My first load is all clothes for Andy. I get one load going in each of the four machines and then head back upstairs. The apartment is empty.

I climb up on top of the milk crate and go out the window.

It's not really a balcony, because there isn't a door to get to it anymore. But it's more than a fire escape. I don't know what you call that.

It's where I watch my collection of VHS movies that have women scientists in them. *Contact. Madame Curie. Gorillas in the Mist.* The TV/VCR combo was one of my luckiest finds ever. VHS tapes are cheap.

When we first came to live here, Mom told us that the best thing about being the apartment manager was getting to take stuff that people leave behind when they move out. I didn't believe her, but it turned out to be true.

For the first few years, I picked Barbies and Andy found toys. But as Mom got worse and came home less, we started taking clothes, blankets, shoes . . . anything else we thought we could use. This TV/ VCR was just in somebody's closet. It works fine.

My stack of VHS tapes is right beside it, ready to go. I put in *Jurassic Park*, my favorite movie to watch when I'm ditching school. I love seeing Dr. Sattler as the smartest person on the island and the one to survive all the way to the end. After the T. rex attacks, I'll go put the clothes in the dryer.

12:32 p.m.

When the laundry's all done, I have the same problem as always: where to put it.

Anything of Mom's gets folded up and put on the couch. She'll sleep right on top of it, most times.

The bottom drawer of Andy's dresser rotted and fell out from getting wet too many times. I don't know what was in it, but whatever it was is all stuck to the floor now with something growing on it. When I open the next drawer, there are four wide brown mushrooms sprouting out of the black wood at the back. That just leaves the top drawer. I stuff everything I can into that and throw the rest on the top.

I don't have a dresser, but the desk under my loft bed has a big drawer that was made to hold files. I can fit all of my clean clothes in it. Looking at my shorts, I'm thinking about fall coming soon. If it gets much colder, Andy and I are both gonna need new coats. Mom will get calls from the school about that, too. I'll start hinting about a trip to Goodwill this weekend.

I head to the kitchen to see if there's anything to eat when I hear a buzz. It's been so long since I heard my cell phone go off that I almost forgot what it sounds like on vibrate. It's the first of the month, so Mom must have made a payment on our plan again.

I run back to my hideout and get to it just in time to answer. I don't know the number on the screen.

"Hello?"

"Hi, Layla. It's Kristi's mom, Bette."

I wait a second before saying anything. "Oh. Hi."

I shouldn't have answered the phone.

"So, Kristi texted me today and told me you're home sick from school."

"Yeah."

"Is your mom home?"

"No." If I bite my nails, can the person on the other end of the call hear it?

"Okay, well, I was going to go shopping, and I wanted to know if you'd come with me. It's really boring to go alone, and I'll take you out to lunch. What do you say?" She's too cheerful. Something is up.

On the one hand, I'm pretty sure I'm gonna have to sit through a lecture of some kind. On the other hand, lunch.

"Uh, sure. Sure, I'll go with you. Do you want me to walk over there?"

"No, sweetie, I'll come pick you up."

"Okay, well, you have to have a controller to get through the gate. I'll stand outside and wait for you." Exactly what my mom tells the pizza guy. The UPS guy. Everyone. To keep them away from our front door.

"Alright, be there in just a minute." Bette says goodbye and hangs up.

I'm halfway to the door before I realize I'm still wearing the clothes she washed for me yesterday. I switch to another outfit from the file drawer and get out there. There's no time to do anything about my hair, but it's not too bad today.

No time at all, and there she is before I make it out of the gate.

"Hi, Layla!"

Kristi's mom drives a big white SUV with tan leather seats that warm up when it starts. It's the nicest car I've ever been in. It smells new, even though they've had it for a year. I slide across the leather and buckle my seat belt. "Hi."

"So, level with me. You're not really sick, are you?"

I look over at her. She's smiling, with her perfect blonde highlights framing her face.

"No, I'm not. I'm playing hooky."

She laughs as she pulls away from the curb. "I did a lot of that in high school. You're a little ahead of yourself for a junior-high kid. But I know you're pretty smart, so it probably doesn't matter."

We drive past the school and I don't even look.

"So how are your grades?"

"Really good." Honor roll every year since there was such a thing. Happy-face stickers on my 100 percent tests before that. Not like Andy, who I have to drag through his weekly reading every Sunday night.

"Yeah? What's your favorite subject?"

"Science."

She drives up the ramp to the freeway, and the seat warms up my back, and it's so nice and so comfortable that I'm sure we're going to crash any minute and that will be the end of it.

"I never liked science. It was too complicated for me. Good for you, girl."

I'm looking straight ahead, but I can feel her looking at me, like glancing over when she feels safe enough to do it.

"So, I wonder if you'll do me a favor."

I'm looking at her without turning my head. Her loose coat made out of cashmere or something. Her big diamond ring flashing in the sun on the leather steering wheel. Sure, she needs a favor from me. Right. Okay.

I don't answer.

"I used to take Kristi shopping, when she was younger. I really loved it, and we'd pick out a first-day-of-school outfit together. We used to get along really well. But now she just uses my card to shop for herself online, which is fine with me, but I really miss the trip. I was wondering if you would let me take you shopping today and get a new outfit, just like Kristi and I used to do. It can be our secret, but I think that'd be really fun. I need to get a few things for me, and then we'll go get some lunch. How's that sound?" She says all this like she doesn't think I'll see right through it.

There's isn't any word for the mix of shame and eagerness I am stuck with right now. It's like a blue-ringed octopus (*Hapalochlaena lunulata*) trying to sting its way out of my chest. I know exactly what she is doing. I don't know if I'm supposed to be grateful that she made up a lie to make me feel better, or if she knows how insulting it is to my intelligence that she doesn't think I get it.

I get it. I want it. What she's offering here. What Kris won't give her, I can give her. It's like an affair, in a weird way. I can't even breathe. I look out the window and count lampposts and try to act normal.

"I guess."

I could tell her that I get it. I could be way nicer to her, if that's what she really misses from Kris. I could be a more grateful charity case.

But if I say any more words now I'm gonna cry. So I swallow hard and take deep breaths until we get to the mall.

She buys herself perfume, a pair of earrings. She doesn't need anything, it's so obvious. She tells the saleslady to measure me for a bra and bring me some choices.

The saleslady is short, with shiny black hair and the kind of old-fashioned bra that makes torpedoes up front. She puts her hands on my back and I jump like a rabbit.

"What?"

"I need to measure you, honey. To find your size." She's talking quietly, like I'm sick or something.

I didn't sign up for this. She takes me into a dressing room and shuts the door behind us.

"If you're comfortable taking your shirt off, I'll get a better measurement that way."

"Sure." I pull my T-shirt over my head and stand there in the only bra I've ever owned. It's rattier than an actual rat—all popped elastic and too small a year ago. I'm waiting for her to laugh at me.

She doesn't laugh. "Arms up, please."

I do as I'm told. She skates along my ribs, and I'm more aware of the smell of my own armpits than I ever have been in my life.

"Not a shaver, eh? My daughter's like that. Thinks body hair is a revolution."

Add that to the list of things I'm supposed to take a razor to.

"Alright, I think you're still a B-cup. Let me bring you some choices."

A minute later, three lacy stupid underwired nightmares come over the top of the door. I don't know how to tell her that I can't wear anything this pretty. It is just not allowed. I try to picture where I would keep it in my house, or how it would look paired with my worn-out shirts and underwear. It just doesn't belong. Wrong phylum. Wrong planet.

I put the beige one on, hoping it won't be ridiculous.

It is.

"Well? How's that working out?" She's right on the other side.

"It's not . . . It doesn't . . . I don't think this is right." I look like I have four boobs. I'm not saying that over the door.

"Let me see."

And then she busts in on me again, clicking her tongue. "Oh, my my my. You're a C-cup already. I think you're luckier than your mother in that department."

"She's not my mother."

"Oh. Alright, then, let me bring you the next size up." She bustles away again.

"Can I . . . Can it please be something less lacy? Like just a plain regular bra?"

"More into clean lines? To wear under T-shirts, I imagine?"

"Yeah. Yeah. These other ones, they . . ." I don't know how to say it.

"They show through, certainly. Just a moment."

She's gone again, and I'm stuck with the me in the mirror. I look carefully at my face, trying to figure out how someone could think I'm Bette's daughter. Maybe her eyesight isn't very good. But at least I don't look too much like Mom. If I looked for me in the mirror and saw her, I'd probably never look again.

I end up with a black one. No stupid lace, no stupid bow, and the short saleslady leaves me alone.

Bette buys me a pack of underwear, and it ends up being two outfits: two new pairs of jeans and two shirts.

"It's so cheap, let's get two. Okay?" Bette's really enjoying this. She wasn't lying about that.

It's on the tip of my tongue to ask her if we can trade it all in for a coat instead, but I don't. She swipes her credit card and I look away, like I can avoid the feeling of it if I just never see a number. I shove the word *charity* out of my head and it drops to the floor. We go get lunch at an Italian place, and I panic about ordering something too expensive. I stare down the menu, trying to figure out what's enough but not too much.

Bette orders for me, and the waiter brings me a peach iced tea.

We're alone, so here it comes.

"Listen, Layla. I think your mom's in a really tough spot right now." She holds a glass of mineral water and kind of rolls it back and forth between her hands. Her nails are painted almost the exact color of her skin. Her ring clinks against the glass when it rolls left. She looks like she's trying hard.

"It must be really difficult to do it alone. I can't imagine what I would have done without Kristi's dad when the girls were little. Or even what I would do now, without Sean. It's really tough to raise kids alone."

I watch the bubbly water rolling. I don't answer, and I don't follow the glass when she takes a sip.

"But you're a good kid. And it's not your fault that your mom doesn't have much time for you. And I just wanted to help a little. I know how mean kids at school can be."

She doesn't have any idea. But she looks like she's pleased with herself, and she deserves that much.

The waiter brings us salads and bread and pasta and cheese and pepper, and setting it all up is like a major deal.

Bette is absorbed in eating for just a few minutes, and I am so grateful. I work my way through everything in front of me, and they keep bringing me more tea. That part of this day could go on forever and that'd be fine. But Bette's talking again.

She takes a deep breath. I put the straw in my mouth and pull and pull and pull.

"You have good grades. You're savvy. You're organized. You could really go somewhere and be something. I just want you to know that. You're not stuck."

She says this like I don't know. Like I haven't been doing the math since I was twelve. Just a few more years until I can move out, get a job, go to college if I beg for help just right. Four years of high school and planning out how I can take Andy with me. Until then, *stuck* is exactly the word.

She delicately pushes her fork into the sliced mushrooms on the edge of her plate, and I think of the ones growing in Andy's dresser drawer.

Enough cold tea down my throat and I can do it. Always braver on a full stomach.

"Thank you. This all really means a lot to me." I sound normal. Fine.

She smiles, and she looks a little like she might cry. I eat the last slice of the bread, wiping my plate clean with it. I'm hoping she'll order dessert, but she leaves half her lunch uneaten on her plate and doesn't mention it. Oh well.

The ride home is quiet, and I hold the bag in both hands the whole way. She pulls up to the gate again to drop me off. "Do you think your mom's home? I could just pop in and explain—"

"No, she works really late. She won't be home for a while yet. Don't worry, I'll explain it to her."

"Well, okay. If you're sure."

She's planning to hug me. I open the car door and swing my legs out, grabbing my one big shopping bag.

"I'm sure. Thank you again, Bette." Can a person die of guilt?

She rolls down the window after I shut the door. "Oh, I forgot. Kristi said to tell you she signed you guys up for some contest with your science teacher. She said she'll text you about it later."

So Kristi knows you're here. So this isn't our little secret. Experiments in trust never seem to produce good results.

"Okay, thanks." I'm already turning to walk away as I say it. Up the stairs quick, and I push the shopping bag in and slide through the window. I pull the new clothes out, to hide them away and calculate how long I can keep them looking new. I leave the bag directly in the middle of the living-room floor, clearing a spot between soda cans and cigarette butts, kicking aside a wet, yellowed T-shirt.

8:20 p.m.

Mom brings home tacos again. I let Andy have them. He grins and there's shredded cheese in his teeth, and I feel that swelling slug in my chest that I can't ever fix this for him. He's sitting on something dry, but surrounded by waterlogged junk. It's never bothered him; Andy doesn't know any better. He shoots the balled-up wrappers into the shopping bag from the mall. It sits up like a bright, gold-edged bucket. The bottom of it is already wet; I can see the inky-gray water crawling up the sides.

Nobody asks where it came from.

That's life.

Thursday 7:30 a.m.

First period is English. Honors English is for some reason a collection of the worst people in this school.

We're reading *Great Expectations*. Well, somebody is reading it. I read it already. It has its moments.

Mrs. Forbes told us we could turn in the midterm essay anytime before winter break. I hope she knows that means she's gonna get like twenty-five papers on December 22. I turned mine in right after Halloween. I wrote about the symbolism of Miss Havisham, the woman who covered all her windows, stopped all her clocks, and lived in her wedding dress with her rotting wedding cake for her whole life after she got left at the altar. I felt like I knew her.

I got an A.

I sit in the last seat on the far side of the classroom, under an open window. It doesn't matter where I sit.

Paul DeMarco breezes past me on his way to the front of the class with his iPad in his hands. "God, it's like a cat pissed on a bag of rotten peanuts."

Ryan Audubon is right behind him. "No, it's more like when my dog eats his own crap and then throws it up and then eats it again and then craps it again."

Emerson Berkeley walks in behind them with his headphones in, doesn't say a word to anybody. He sits in the front corner of the room. Kristi says he has this theory that it's the easiest place for the teacher to overlook.

Paul and Ryan don't directly address me, so we can all pretend this isn't happening. I can look out the window and wait for Paul to get distracted by his iPad, or for Ryan to show him something on his phone, or for the two of them to focus on anything else.

But when Jane Chase comes in, I know my time pretending no one is talking to me is over.

"Layla, can I ask you something?" Her eyebrows are plucked so thin they're like a single hair each. Her perfect hair, her shark smile. I could kill her a thousand times.

"Can't stop you."

"How do you get your hair to do that? I try to rat mine up to look like a scene kid or whatever, and no matter what I use it won't stay." She leans her cheek against her hand and stares at me.

"Natural talent." I'm waiting for Amber Rodin or Mackenzie Biros to show up; they usually travel in a pack. People trickle through the door, but not those two.

"Really? There's no trick to it? Like I want it super tangly, like yours. And then like really greasy at the roots, but then super dry at the ends. It can't just naturally be like that. You must be doing something. Please, teach me your secrets." She's just barely not laughing. Her phone's not out this time. She's not recording, so I have no idea what she's getting out of this. There isn't even anybody around to laugh.

No, wait. There's Mackenzie.

"Jane, come on. The bell's gonna ring." Mackenzie has a new leather jacket, in a really pretty shade of light blue-green. I almost want to tell her how much I like it.

Amber brings up the rear, running her fingers through her big curly hair to pull it all over to one side of her head. I should be asking her this question—I'd give anything to know how she does that. Her hair is almost as curly as mine. But it's so shiny and long, and she can pull her hand right through it. I stare and stare.

"What?" Amber stares back at me, her green eyes narrow.

I look away.

Mackenzie is dragging Jane by her sleeve as the bell finally rings. I watch Amber's hair as she settles a few rows ahead of me. Jane and Mackenzie laugh about something and I'm not even here. In my head, I'm in my hideout. I'm safe.

Mrs. Forbes reads a piece of my essay in her lecture today about *Great Expectations*. She doesn't tell them it's mine.

I'm so relieved.

1:44 p.m.

As soon as Mr. Raleigh tells us we can break into groups, Kristi comes and sits on the stool next to me.

"So my mom told you about the contest?" She is really committed to this black look. She has way too much eyeliner on. She looks like a raccoon.

"Yeah, but she didn't say what the contest was, just that you wanted to do it."

"Okay, so. We sign up to use one of the school's cameras. They're really good cameras, they got them from some company who just gave them to the school. The assignment is to find a really unusual biome here in our own town. So like a little bit of grass on the freeway median with a few bugs in it or whatever."

"Okay, yeah. We could do that. Do you have any ideas?"

"Yeah, the freeway thing. I *just* said it. Are you even listening?" She looks up from her black nails, already pissed at me.

"Oh, I thought that was just like an example. Not your actual idea. So how do we sign up?"

"I already signed us up. We're a team. So like you go film the biome and identify what's in it and then bring it to me. I have Final Cut Pro on my Mac, so I'll do the editing and add music and credits and all that. It'll look awesome!"

"Okay. Okay, let's do it."

Mr. Raleigh shows up right on time. "Alright, ladies. Did you figure out what you're going to film?"

"Yeah, we got it." I check his black eyes for the expression of anxious pity. He's looking Kristi over, instead. As if her new makeup is the concern of the week now.

"Kristi, all clear on the project guidelines?"

"Yeah. When do we get cameras?"

"You'll get permission slips today, and you can take a camera home when it's signed and returned."

I'm not even worried about it. Mom's signature has never been a problem.

4:05 p.m.

"Both of our moms have to sign it. It says that, right here."

While she walks home, Kristi is trying to shoot a video of herself that shows off all her possible facial expressions in ten seconds.

"Okay, fine. Fine, I'll get it signed."

She's trying to look worried, but she wants to look worried and still pretty. It seems like a hard job.

"So I'll get my mom to sign mine tonight."

Andy is right at my heels. "You're gonna have Mom sign it? For real?"

"Yes, just like she signed your field-trip slip last month," I say through clenched teeth. I give him the pinch that is supposed to shut him up, but it doesn't.

"You're gonna get a camera so you can do a naked-lady show!" He puts his hands on his hips and does a weird little wiggle dance.

"Yes, I'm gonna make a naked-lady show. You're so stupid, Andy."

He puckers up his lips and makes kissy noises at me. He gets away too quick for me to kick him.

Kristi's yelling, "God, I hate you! I can't stand you! You're disgusting!"

We both turn to look at her, but she's acting for her phone again.

"So if we get our permissions in tomorrow, we can start filming after school," I say, just to get her to focus.

"Maybe I should do the narrating." She's rewatching the video of herself.

"What? Why?"

"I'm a really good actor. I could give it some drama, you know?" She makes the word *drama* just a little too long.

"I guess, but you don't know what anything is."

She turns her screen off finally and slips the phone into her pocket. "Okay, but you could film it and then write a script, and then I could be, like, the actor. And then edit it on my computer and make it look really pretty."

"So I'm just, like, a camera person, then? I get all the work and you get all the fun stuff?"

"Writing the definitions down is fun!"

I give her the best eye roll I can manage. We cross the street, not talking.

"Editing is hard work, too. And I *have* to do it, because you don't even have a computer," Kristi says, as if she's the victim in all this.

I can feel my cheeks getting hot. "I can do it on one of the school computers. And you can do your own stupid homework. I don't know why I always get stuck doing all the crap on our projects while you do drawings on the cover, or the acting. It's not even fair."

"Layla. Layla. Layla. I want a donut, Layla. Buy me a donut." Andy is patting me with one sticky hand, pointing at the donut shop.

"Leave me alone, Andy."

"Fine, then I'll do the project myself. Since you're being such a bitch about it. And you can use one of the crappy school computers," Kristi says.

"Fine. And you can try and figure out what those little squiggles in the textbook mean. They're called words, by the way."

"Ugh. I can see why my mom feels sorry for you. Here." She pulls two dollars out of her pocket and gives them to Andy. "So you can get a donut. Since I know you're . . . whatever."

Andy's so excited about a donut, he runs off without even saying thanks. He's still too little to really feel humiliation.

Are my eyes fire right now? My eyes feel like fire and my face is red-hot metal.

I think of a million awful things to say. I think of every curse word I have ever heard, of telling her that no one likes her because she's a conceited bitch and that redheads don't have souls.

I don't say anything.

I walk fast toward the gate. I can't even stand being close enough to hear her. But when she starts laughing, I hear that.

"Jane Chase just tweeted about you. I think I'll tweet her back."

I walk away fast before I say something I can't unsay. This has happened before.

She'll be back.

Coming through the window, I can hear my mother moving around in there. It's too late to turn back—she knows I'm home.

Mom's standing on the edge of the kitchen, right where the living-room carpet starts.

She's got a big black trash bag in one hand, and she's smoking with the other. Her clothes look like they're hanging off of her. Her eyes are too deep in her face. It looks like she dyed her hair earlier today—it's

41

crazy red, like a clown or a cartoon character. Oh shit. All the signs. I hope Andy hangs out at the donut shop for a long time.

"Will you look at this place?"

I don't say anything.

She picks up huge handfuls of everything: A glass jar with moldy spaghetti sauce running down one side. Gray socks. Wet newspaper. Chicken bones.

"This is unbelievable. I work all day and this is what I come home to? How am I supposed to make dinner? I can't live like this."

You haven't made dinner in months.

I don't say anything.

She finds that banana that I slid one foot through a couple of days ago, black and crawling with tiny flies. "Can't you see this? Don't you know this place needs to be cleaned up?"

Her voice is rising. I hope she gets this one out of her system fast. I really need to go to school tomorrow.

"Well? Why are you just standing there? Get a bag."

I walk over to the giant box of giant bags and pull one off the spool. I sink down and start filling it blindly, with whatever I find when I put my hand down. I shove it full and open another.

"Don't just set it down! Take it out to the dumpster."

I know better than to offer resistance. I push the bag through the window and follow it out. I walk it down to the dumpster by the gate and I wait as long as I can, hoping to catch Andy on his way in and warn him. When time runs out, I jog back up.

"How the hell could that take you so long?" She's sitting on the couch, pulling up soda cans and magazines and takeout boxes from the moat she makes around herself when she won't get off it. "This couch smells like pee. Has your little brother been peeing here? Is he that lazy?"

The couch smells like pee because you lay on it not moving for almost nine days last month. Those were bad days. You didn't eat. If you had stopped drinking the minimum amount of water to keep a human body alive, I would have had to get help, and I didn't know who I would call. But you kept drinking water, and you did eventually get up. You started talking again.

I don't say anything.

"Go empty the bucket in the bathroom."

I go right away and suck the hose to drain the bucket into the bathtub. I'm still in there when I hear Andy come through the window. Damn it.

Out in the living room, he's already crying, sitting on the floor with a garbage bag. He doesn't know about not answering yet.

"I'm sorry, Mommy."

"I brought you all those tacos. I got you that cereal you like and I put a roof over your head, and you can't even help me keep the house from falling apart." She's standing right over him, waving her arms.

"I'm sorry, Mommy, I'm sorry."

She won't quit. She bends down and picks up an empty juice bottle. "How long has it been since you had this kind of juice?"

"A long time." He can't even catch his breath.

"Then how can it still be on the floor?" She's screaming now. "How can you live like this?"

She stomps into the kitchen. I've seen this a hundred times, but she has never made the mistake of opening the fridge. No one is allowed to open the fridge. She tenses up like a cat hissing if you even go near it. She opens the door wide and stands there a minute before she throws up all over the floor.

The fridge went bad sometime around Easter, which was six months ago. I know the ham is still in there. I think there was chicken in the freezer. Definitely there was milk. The rest I don't remember. The power went off the Monday after Easter, and Mom said not to open it, to keep everything cold until the power came back on.

But that took almost two weeks. So everything went bad slowly, in the dark with the door closed. The few times it's been opened since then, the smell has been something intensely awful. Not like bad eggs, not like spoiled milk. Not like a dumpster, not like poop. Not even like all those things put together. It's not like anything at all.

I can't get close, but I go to the edge of the kitchen and I can see. It's all black and green in there; the black is slick and wet while the green is thick and furry. Parts of it are moving, and I know that those are maggots. She slams the door. I'm hoping that took the fight out of her.

It didn't.

She gets under the kitchen sink and finds a bottle of something. She takes the cap off and starts pouring it over where she's thrown up, which is mostly boxes of expired Hamburger Helper she had stacked against the wall of the kitchen, and some spilled cereal. She pours it all over, splashing up and down the kitchen floor. Roaches stream out as the cleaning stuff drips through.

"Where's the mop? I'm going to mop this floor." She looks all around the room.

I don't think we have one. I can't remember what the kitchen floor looks like. I don't say anything.

Andy is quietly throwing up in his trash bag. When he's done, he goes back to filling it. He knows better than I thought.

Friday 2:38 a.m.

She stops yelling around midnight, after she takes the third noise complaint by phone from one of the tenants nearby. I hear her saying she'll go over to the apartment making the noise and give them a talking to, threaten to call the cops.

I wish somebody would.

She stops having Andy take bags of trash out the window when someone almost sees him.

I wish somebody had.

We did make a dent. We got most of the wet newspaper out of the hallway. There's a path through the living room, and a lot of the kitchen is cleared out. I can see black mold blooming up one wall in the bathroom, now that Mom took all the old towels out of there and bagged them up to be washed later. I'm just gonna throw them away when she's not here. I know how that will end.

We both know we're not allowed to quit until she says we can.

She realizes she's out of cigarettes and is gonna wake up without one. "I guess you two can go to bed now. I know you won't keep working once I'm gone. I can't expect that much from you. That's way too much to ask."

Andy gets up immediately, tying up his bag, so tired he can hardly stand. "Okay, good night, Mommy. I'm sorry. I love you."

She doesn't say anything.

She goes through the window, barefoot and wordless. I take a deep breath.

"Andy, wash your hands before you go to bed. There's soap in the kitchen."

He goes to do it and I follow him. We both wash up and climb into bed. I'm hoping he'll just pass out, but he's full of questions.

"Why does she get like this?"

"I don't know."

"Where does she go when she leaves?" He's mumbling now.

"Work, most of the time."

"What about at night?"

"I don't know." I really don't.

"Where do you go when you leave?"

"Not far. Just out," I tell him.

"Is this gonna happen again tomorrow?"

"I don't know. Probably not. Remember, last time it only lasted a day. And it's been a while."

"Yeah."

"Go to sleep, Andy."

"I love you, Layla."

I don't say anything.

Friday 6:00 a.m.

Here's the problem: Andy won't get up. Three hours of sleep isn't enough for anybody. Even if I'm willing to give it a shot, he's not.

If I don't go to science today, I can't get my permission slip in to borrow a camera until Monday. The project is due next Friday, and I want to have the weekend to get some filming done. If I go to school during lunch, I can slip into my afternoon classes.

Mom's asleep on the couch. Staying home is not an option.

Getting Andy dressed when he's this tired is the worst. He's limp, he's whiny, and he lies back down if I turn away for one second. I get him into a pair of pants and pinch him for trying to lie down again.

He starts to cry for real, and I grab his face in both hands. "She's asleep on the couch, you moron. Shut up!"

He shuts his mouth, but his little baby tears go on.

I finally get myself dressed, and we tiptoe past her together. She's turned toward the back of the couch, facing away from us. We go out the window as quietly as we can. She doesn't even stir.

"Okay, listen. Listen. Are you listening?"

He's sniffling and looking away from me as obviously as possible.

I grab his shoulder hard and turn him toward me.

"Do you want to listen to me and get more sleep, or do you want to be a butthole?"

He looks up at me, his eyes red and his nose running.

Roughly, I wipe his nose with the edge of my sleeve. "Don't go to your classroom. Go to the nurse's office and tell her your teacher sent you. Okay?"

"Okay."

"Tell the nurse you have a headache. Not a tummy ache, not anything else. A headache. Say it."

"I have a headache."

"Okay, good. The nurse will call Mom, but Mom won't answer. Tell her you don't want to go home, you just want to lie down for a while. Get up at lunchtime and tell her you feel better. Eat lunch and then go to class. Tell your teacher you had a doctor's appointment. Okay? Say it."

"I had a doctor 'poitmet." He's wiping his own nose now.

"Right. The nurse will turn the light off and let you sleep, as long as you don't bother her or say the wrong thing, or cry like a stupid baby. Can you handle that?"

He doesn't answer, but he walks a little farther away from me.

"What if Mom does answer?"

I don't say anything.

My eyes feel like I just pulled them out of a microwave. The nurse's office won't work for me, I know that. At the beginning of the year, she was all sweet and concerned and giving me free pads from the sample box. Now she's always telling me to go back to class and stop abusing the privilege.

I'm going to have to use one of my riskier hideouts.

I drop Andy at school and walk off like I'm going through the park to my junior high. Instead, I head down one of the side streets.

It's not quite light out yet. The brown mountains are lined with the glow of sunrise, but the sun hasn't cleared them yet. I still have a little time.

The last time I used this hideout was back in February. Mom had a big box of chocolates, and close to the end of the month she opened the box to find that most of them were gone. I honestly don't know if Andy ate them or she ate them herself and then forgot about it. What I do know is that I didn't touch a single one of her fucking chocolates. But I was the only one home when she found it.

I woke up to her screaming, and like an idiot I came down the ladder to find out what was wrong. I had barely come around the doorway when the box hit me in the face. The two heart-shaped halves came apart in the air, and the last few candies flew out and pelted me, falling down my chest. The top of the box left a tiny cut in my forehead, and I just stood there, blinking.

"Can't I have anything—just *one thing*—that you don't get into? Do you have to get into everything that's mine? I just wanted some *fucking chocolate*." Her eyes were so narrow they were like tiny pinches into the dough of her skin. Spit flew out of her mouth. I could see the cords in her neck pulsing, and I wanted so badly to just make them stop, just make her stop, to never wake up to this again.

She went on like that for a while, but my ears were ringing and I couldn't hear her anymore. I climbed out the window while she was still screaming, in my pj's and with no shoes on. I don't know what my plan was, but I found this place that night.

This block is mostly old people. It's not as nice as Kristi's, or the ones on the other side of the school where a bunch of the teachers live. There are old cars sitting on flat tires in driveways, and people have sheets hung up as curtains in the windows. That first time, I knew I would be safe here.

One house has sheets on all its windows except for one with a big faded American flag, right in the middle. In the driveway, penned in by a car, there's an old motor home with a door on the opposite side of the house. The night of the chocolates, I found the door unlocked. It's been that way every time since.

Four flat tires, and the thing is packed with junk. I can hear mice shredding the old magazines and seat cushions to make their nests. Up above the driver's seat, there's a kind of attic. A foam mattress and a pillowcase-and-blanket set with cowboys and Indians all over it. It looks old.

I climb in and shake everything, checking for mice. Any *Peromyscus californicus*? After a minute nothing moves, so I settle under the blanket and lie very still for a little while.

The first time I got in here, I couldn't sleep at all. I just lay in here, shaking. I don't know if I was mad or sad or afraid of getting caught. I waited all day, and then finally slept at night. I heard the car pull in and people go into the house. I never even moved. I stayed there for two days, until I was too hungry to stay any longer.

Mom never asked me where I had gone. I wouldn't have told her.

So today, the old yellow RV windows are slowly lighting up, and the mice are rustling, and the neighborhood is quiet. I fall asleep almost right away. I can't believe how quickly this starts to feel normal.

Noon

My phone buzzes to wake me up, and I turn it off before its second vibration. Not moving, I listen hard to find out if anyone is around the RV. Emerging in the middle of the day is pretty risky—I prefer to come and go when it's dark.

I slide out of the little attic and peek through the window that faces out. Seems clear.

I slip out and latch the door. I walk around the front of the RV and straight into the mailman.

I make a little squeaky noise and bounce off the tall man's chest.

"Whoa, hey! Sorry about that." He peers into his bag and walks past me. My heart is pounding so hard that I can see it if I look down at my shirt.

Shake that off. Get to school.

I make it to school too late to get any lunch, so I just head over to Mr. Raleigh's class.

Kristi's already in there.

She's sitting slumped at her desk, and she doesn't look up when I walk in. Raleigh's at his desk, so I head over to him.

"Mr. Raleigh?"

He looks up from smiling at his crotch.

"Hey, can I give you my permission slip now to get a camera? I don't want to be late for my next class." I am not going to look back at Kristi. I am not.

"Well, if I let you have a camera now, you have to promise me you won't fiddle with it during class."

No, I'll just fiddle with my phone, like everyone else.

"I promise." I pull the folded permission slip out of my pocket and hand it over.

Kristi comes up behind me, holding hers. Raleigh puts a slick little video camera into my hand and follows it with a little neoprene case.

"Keep it in there at all times. If you're not filming, it's in the case."

"Got it."

Kristi hands over her paper. "I'm going to film a freeway meridian, to see what lives there." She says it just a little bit too loud.

"Good idea, Kristi."

Yeah, amaze everybody with some Coccinellidae. Ladybugs. Exciting.

When she turns around with her camera in its little case, I can see that she's been crying. She looks at me just long enough to see I'm looking at her, and then away. Okay, then.

We slog through class, but between almost everyone holding a camera and Raleigh's obvious distraction, it seems like we don't really get anything done. The bell rings, and I head to Honors English.

Jane and Mackenzie are both tweeting when we walk in. Phones beep and buzz all over the room, and there's a lot of low laughter and people make eye contact across the rows.

I quit looking at anybody. I know this is about me. It's always about me.

I sit in my usual spot against the wall and wait for the bell to ring so that they have to stop.

"There she is."

It's Jane's voice, confident and sure and so mean that it stings. I look up and they're all watching Kristi walk in.

She's trying to ignore them, but she's not doing a great job. She comes and sits beside me.

"They're all assholes. You were totally right about that, at least." Kristi sounds like she's been crying.

"Oh, are we talking again?" I keep looking out the window.

"Come on, Layla. At least just talk to me until the bell rings. I need a way to ignore them."

She sounds sad enough that I actually look.

"What are they bothering you about?"

She leans way over the desk to get close to me, and she whispers. "I tweeted my poem last night. Jane figured out who I was talking about and retweeted it at him. They've all been making fun of me since then. Emerson didn't answer, but it doesn't matter. Assholes."

"I'm sorry, Kristi." I'm a little sorry. I'm a little sure that she got about what she deserved. And I'm so glad that this time it wasn't me.

She's still leaning. "Can I come over after school today? I really just need to get away." She looks so sad I can barely stand it.

For half a second I think about my RV hideout. "I really can't have anybody over, Kris. It isn't personal. We could go to the library. Or hang out at the park."

She slips back into her chair, folding her arms. The bell rings.

Outside, I can't find Andy. I walk home alone.

4:15 p.m.

Andy's there waiting for me.

"They called Mom. She did answer. You were wrong."

I flop down onto the couch, kicking over a soda can. "So?"

"So Mom told them to let me walk home. The nurse yelled at her."

I can totally breathe normally. Respiration. Exhalation. I'm fine.

"What did she yell at her?"

"I dunno. A bunch of big words."

"Did you walk home?"

"Yeah," he says. He still sounds tired.

Not like there was another option. Not like we have a car.

"Was Mom here?"

"No."

I make us each a package of ramen. Mom comes home before they're finished cooking.

"I hope you're happy now."

I'm not even turning around.

"You knew the nurse would call me. She woke me up. Ranting at me about some bullshit. Why did you send him to school? He could have just slept in, we both could have."

"I didn't know if today was going to be a bad day for you." I turn off the fire.

She's quiet for a minute.

"It's a bad day for me now."

I wish she sounded sad. I wish she was sorry. I wish I could tell that she felt anything other than inconvenienced.

Also, that wasn't what I meant, and she knows it. But I don't know what words I should use. There aren't any words for a lot of things.

"Well, it's the weekend. He has a couple of days before he has to go back. That should fix it," I tell her cautiously. I don't want to set her off.

"It better. I don't need any more shit from his school." She's headed to the couch, and even though she's one person and there are four seats, there's nowhere to sit.

I drain the bucket in the bathroom and run myself a bath. I'm in it with a book when I notice the spider behind the toilet. It's graceful and strange, working on its web. I can't identify it from here; it's a little too small.

I start to wonder whether anyone else's house has ever had this kind of biodiversity inside of it. My house is really like its own planet, with different biospheres. Swamps of wet newspaper growing exotic fungi. An enclosed jungle of teeming green life in the dead fridge. Fruit flies and tiny worms and the occasional mouse and this spider, just a few inches away from my face. Do any other humans live like this? Was this what it was like to be Dr. Jane Goodall, living with the chimps she studied?

I'm considering the advantage of living in my own personal petri dish when the lights go out.

Perfect.

By the time I pull the plug and walk out with my clothes stuck to me, she's gone and Andy is trying to light a candle. I light it for him and take him to bed. It's not even dark outside yet, but I am done with the day.

I lie there trying to hold it together until the day is done with me.

Saturday 8:30 a.m.

I remember the day we moved into this apartment.

It had been a little while since we had a real apartment. After the sheriff staple-gunned the notice to the front door, we'd moved out of the last place fast.

Mom came to my bed in the middle of the night and told me to pick the most important things that were mine and put them in my backpack. I figured my school stuff was most important, and I packed some clothes around my books and pencils. I lost my hairbrush and most of my underwear that day. I've been planning since then how to do it right next time. Andy filled a bag with stuffed animals. I got yelled at for that later, even though I had no idea.

We walked up the road for what seemed like hours. Mostly toward the grocery store, the one you could take carts from without the wheels locking down. A block or two before that, we turned and arrived at the Valencia Inn.

I was twelve when we came to live at the Valencia, but I already knew a lot about it. We had been kicked out of three other apartment complexes in this town, but at least we didn't live in this broke-down hotel. At least I had that over a few kids at school.

But here we were.

We only stayed at the Valencia for a couple of months, but it was long enough to get lice. Twice. Andy got his head shaved, but Mom said if we did that to my hair, she would get in trouble.

My hair is nothing but trouble, so that didn't surprise me.

It's always been kinky-curly, rough and ugly, and impossible to take care of. It's not like Mom's, not like Andy's, not like any human hair I've ever seen. It's like the hair on the dolls I'd find in bins at the thrift store: all matted into one gummy piece and unbrushable. It's been a long time since that day in the bathtub with the knives, but it's never easy. And it's impossible to hide; we're not allowed to wear hats at school, and I'm very jealous of those girls who wear veils.

So when I got lice, Mom came home from the drugstore with a bag of special shampoo and a tiny metal comb and told me to sit in the bath until I had all the little eggs out. I cried until my bathwater was cold, then I rinsed with the vinegar she gave me. It stung in the places where the metal comb had poked my scalp, and the noises I made brought pounding from two different walls.

Two weeks later I got sent home. Again. For lice. Again. *Pediculus humanus capitis.* They're real survivors.

I don't think we really got rid of the lice until we left that hotel. Mom just dyed her hair, over and over, saying it would kill the bugs. The edges of her ears and forehead were purplish red for days, but she never seemed to itch. The day we left, the cops had taped off most of the parking lot.

I don't know how my mom got the job here as an apartment manager. The last job she had was at a burger place. I remember hiding in the back office of the restaurant with Andy, on days when she couldn't pay a babysitter. I remember being home alone after she got told she couldn't do that anymore. But being home alone was better, even if it meant no hot little boxes of fries. Because we finally had our own place again, once she started as a manager here.

In the beginning, there was new furniture (well, new to us) and a few new clothes. There were hot baths, and Mom cooked dinner in the kitchen and slept in her own room.

And then she did the worst thing I can remember.

She sat us down at the little breakfast nook in the kitchen and made us some pancakes. She was all cleaned up, with her hair brushed and her eyes bright. She could really look normal sometimes, I have to remind myself of that. She stood across from us on the other side of the bar. I remember the feeling of her looking at our faces.

"I know that in the past, our house has always gotten dirty. I will need your help with that, both of you, because I have to work a lot of hours. But if you'll help me, I promise it won't get that way again. Okay, guys? I promise that we can do this. We can make this place our real home, just like I always wanted it to be. Okay?"

"Okay, Mommy." Andy was shoveling pancakes into his face. He believed anything she said. He believed her when she said she wouldn't leave us alone again for three days and go to Vegas. He believed her when she said we'd never see *that* boyfriend again. He believed her last time when she said this house would be different.

I hadn't believed her when she'd said that the Valencia was only temporary, though. And it was. So maybe. Maybe I could choose to believe again.

"Okay, Mom."

She smiled then, showing her broken and rotted-out teeth on top and bottom. And I knew I chose wrong.

It didn't happen all at once. It didn't go from sitcom mom and pancakes to the way it is now. Little by little, things fell apart. The door broke, and Mom said we couldn't let maintenance in until the kitchen was cleaned up. But then the fridge went bad and the kitchen went with it. Then the bathroom sink, which meant the carpet got flooded, which meant the newspapers and the mold and the stink. Little things caused big things, and picking up the living room just didn't matter to anyone.

And Mom would be fine one week, bringing home takeout and chain-smoking on the couch, laughing at the TV, but then she'd disappear. Or stop speaking or moving for a few days. Or flip out at us about the house.

A house like this doesn't happen by accident, but as a series of contributing events. Like the forming of an ecosystem. And that's how I start the narration for my video.

Filming is hard. I have to hold a flashlight in one hand and the camera with the other. Even with a window open and candles lit, it isn't enough. The flashlight beam crawls up the mushrooms in Andy's dresser, making their shadows long like giants behind them.

"Here we see a member of the fungus kingdom, genus and species unknown. Here's the cap, the stalk, the gills that hold the reproductive spores, and the volva here at the bottom." I remember the parts from a diagram we filled out in class.

I pan the camera over the big blooms of black mold.

"Here we see a good example of *Stachybotrys*, or black mold. It's associated with sometimes-toxic poor indoor air quality. Like most molds, this needs a lot of moisture and can't survive in direct sunlight."

I looked up the name on Wikipedia, but I might be saying it wrong. Still, I love knowing the Latin or Greek names of a thing. It makes me feel like an actual scientist. I say them in my head, all the time. Feels like I understand something, like I have power during just the length of those syllables.

I follow scuttling roaches and find a spider and a few beetles by the back windows. "*Periplaneta Americana*, the common American cockroach, and *Rosalia funebris*, a borer beetle that I can identify by the banding on its thorax. Both from class Insecta. And here, luckily, we have *Parasteatoda tepidariorum*, a common house spider, who feeds on these insects and helps keep them from taking over everything."

I hold my breath a few minutes and throw open the fridge, focusing in tight on a writhing mass of maggots and the cloud of gnats. No narration there. Too bad.

"The only primate in this biome right now is me. *Homo sapiens*, the smartest thing on two legs." I film my feet, sinking into the gray swamp of newspaper, with the black water rising around my toes. I set the camera down on the sink and film myself siphoning the bucket water into the tub and then set it down again in the kitchen to show how I forage for food. *Opportunistic feeder. Omnivorous primate.* Delicious long words that mean we eat whatever we can find.

The whole thing is five minutes long, and I bet with editing it could be even shorter. I can't possibly turn this in. But it is my ecosystem. And it feels good to make a record of it. It feels like the day I took the knife to my hair. It feels like science. I was actually proving something, actually making a change. I have something unique here, and I have the unique ability to describe it.

I climb into my hiding place and rewatch the footage until the battery starts to die. That brings me to the next project of the day.

With the power out, there is nothing to do in this house. I send Andy to the pool, knowing that on a Saturday there will be other families there and it won't be obvious that he's alone. Once he's gone, I go downstairs to the laundry room and wait for the old woman in there to pull her clothes out of the dryer.

Behind the bank of dryers, deep in the lint fluff and dust, is an extension cord. I cram my arm back there and pull it out. Quick as I can, I tie a loop in the end and throw it up and over the railing of the balcony where my hiding place is. I only miss once. I go back upstairs and through the window, back to my spot. I plug the camera into the other end of the extension and let it charge. Once it's green again, I can watch a movie for a while.

I need to pick another ecosystem to film. I need to delete this one. But I can't. Not yet. Right? Right.

1:30 p.m.

I wish when my phone buzzed that it would be someone cool. It could be Emerson Berkeley, wanting to talk books again, like we did that one time on the field-trip bus. It could even be Kristi, I wouldn't care. I kind of miss her.

But no. It's Kristi's mom, Bette.

Hey, I'm going to go get coffee. Do you want to go?

Yes, but I'd rather you were somebody else. That's a mean answer to someone who is offering to buy me expensive coffee.

Sure. Kristi coming, too?

No, she's not talking to me. Like 15 mins?

Yes. I'll be outside.

I hide the camera behind my TV and leave it plugged in. I'm wearing mostly the clothes Bette bought me, so no problem there. I find my shoes and head on down.

The pretty white car pulls up in no time, and we're rolling toward coffee.

"How are you doing?" She's giving me concern-face.

"I'm fine. Having a lazy Saturday, since all my schoolwork is done. Reading some books. Cleaning up my room."

I am a champion of acting normal.

When I've got a huge whipped-cream-covered coffee drink in my hands, Bette actually starts to talk.

"So, Kristi and I had a fight last night."

"I'm sorry," I say between slurps.

"Yeah, well, it was kind of about you." She pushes her perfect high-lights behind her ear and shrugs at me.

"About me?"

"Yeah. So Kristi was telling me about some trouble she's been having lately, with some of the mean girls at your school."

"Oh yeah, I know the ones." Big sweet swallow.

"She told me they were pretty brutal to her, but that she tried to get them off her back by making fun of you," she says softly.

I don't say anything. She's watching me closely.

"But in the end they got way too mean about it and were planning some kind of prank to humiliate you. She . . . she's not always very considerate, my Kris. But she did stand up for you, when the chips were down." Bette's looking at me like she needs something. Her eyes are sad but still kind of eager. Like I should forgive her, maybe. I don't have any idea why that would matter.

Kris should have sold me out. It would make her life easier, to have some cooler friends. And it wouldn't have mattered to me. What could they possibly do to me? I'm already nothing.

"That was nice of her." What's more worthless than *nice*?

That's what Bette wanted, though. She smiles a little and drinks her black coffee from her fancy reusable cup. She must come here all the time.

"I told her that was the right thing to do, and that those girls should feel terrible, making fun of you for being homeless."

My ears are ringing. "What?"

"Honey, it's okay. You don't have to try to hide it." She reaches across the table and takes my hand. Her skin is soft, and her nails are perfect. Her perfume seems to rise out of the folds of her jacket when she moves. I am not even human. Sudden downgrade from *H. sapiens*.

How can I get out of here without screaming? The door is crowded with people lined up to get coffee. She's holding my hand.

"I'm not . . . why would you think that . . . ?"

"It's fairly obvious. You work very hard to keep it from people. You're such a fighter. Kris told me about sample day."

Samples came on the first day of junior high. We got a lecture from our gym teacher about showers and how we'd start to stink. We got a bag of freebies from some company: a short and stubby deodorant, a free toothbrush, and a pamphlet about our changing bodies and what we can buy to fix them.

I was glad to have a new toothbrush—the one I had at home was way old. But I had never used deodorant before. I had seen it on TV, but I'd never had one. I didn't know when I was supposed to start using it; I thought it was maybe just for adults. I made the mistake of saying that to Kris out loud.

The look on her face was something I never want to see again.

After the sample was gone, I started buying it at the dollar store.

"She told me that she's never been to your house, and how you sometimes look like you haven't slept at all. She says you have to take care of your baby brother all the time."

I can't drink any more of this. My stomach is full of snakes. *Python regius. Dendroaspis polylepis. Agkistrodon piscivorus.*

"So when I finally put it all together, I realized this must be the answer."

"I'm not homeless," I say, trying to make the idea sound ridiculous.

She sighs a little. "Just because you have a little space in an abandoned building, or a shed or something—"

"No. We live in an apartment. My mom is an apartment manager."

Her perfect eyebrows twitch up a little bit. "You don't have to lie to me, sweetie. I know it's embarrassing. But you guys need help."

I stare past her, out to the line of people blocking the door.

"Kristi is mad at me because I told her we have to do something. She doesn't want me to embarrass you or get you in trouble. But, Layla, sweetie, I have to tell somebody. You have to let me get you some help."

"We have an apartment. It has two bedrooms. We've lived there for more than a year."

She looks me dead in the eye. "Then take me to it. I'd like to speak to your mother, anyway."

"I'll take you to my mother." This is the worst idea I have ever had.

"Great." She's already up, swinging her big beige purse over her shoulder. "Let's do that."

I dump my mostly full coffee in the trash. My mouth tastes like caramel bile. How hard is it to jump out of a moving car?

I tell her to park in the spot marked "Future Tenants" right beside the office. Through the big sliding glass door, I can see Mom with her feet up on the desk, reading a paperback and smoking. Bette opens the door.

"You smoke in your office? Is that legal?"

Great opener.

Mom looks up without putting the book down. "Are you a cop?"

Bette stands up a little straighter and walks toward the desk with her hand out.

"My name is Elizabeth Sanderson. Our daughters go to school together. I was hoping we could talk about Layla."

Mom does not even look at me.

"Okay." She pulls her legs off the desk and puts down what she's reading. "What would you like to talk about?" She folds her hands together and leans forward a little.

Oh god. Here we go.

Bette is scared. I can read that like I can read Andy's books. It's so simple and so clear it doesn't even need words.

"Well, I . . . I hardly know where to begin. Layla is a bright girl. In all the gifted classes. She won the spelling bee two years ago, I remember that."

"I know that. I was there," Mom says.

No she wasn't.

63

"Well, I mean, look at the way she comes to school. Her hair is an awful rat's nest, and her clothes are filthy. Did you know she bathes at my house? I thought . . . I thought maybe she was living on the street." Bette looks over her shoulder like she's guilty, like she wants to know whether I heard that or not. When she sees my face, she gets an inch shorter.

Every word is like a needle in me. I know what I look like. I don't want to stand here, but I can't walk away. I have to know what Mom will say.

"She's not living on the street. She's just a lazy, dirty little teenage brat. I can't give her a bath like she's a baby."

Oh, okay. That makes this all my fault.

Bette takes a deep breath. "I'm sorry to be so blunt, I'm just upset. I wanted to help her—to help you, really. If you don't have anywhere to go, there are shelters here in town that prioritize women with children."

Mom sits silent for a moment. Her eyes are like a shark's. "You realize that you're in a rental office right now, right? You think I run this place and don't even have an apartment for my children to live in?"

Bette stutters a little. "I don't know what to think."

Shark eyes never waver. "I think you need to mind your own business, Mrs. Sanderson."

I'm hot all over, but I shake like I'm cold. I want to get in Bette's car and never go home. I'll live in her laundry room and not say a word.

"Mrs. Bailey—"

"That's not my name. That's Layla's name. Not mine."

I have heard that speech so many times. It's really important to her that Andy and I are Baileys and she's not.

"Darlene, then. Isn't that right?"

Mom doesn't say anything.

"Mona Monroe is a friend of mine. She's the on-call nurse over at Maxfield Elementary? She told me that your little boy, Andrew, has all the same problems. He's little enough that you can give him a bath, so why don't you? Why does he show up to school dirty and exhausted? Why is he so hungry that they catch him eating out of the garbage cans once a week?"

Oh shit. I never told him not to do that. It never even occurred to me. Kids have no pride.

"I'm pretty sure I can get her fired for even discussing that with you." The shark never stops swimming, even when it sleeps. *Carcharodon carcharias.*

Bette tries one last time. "Please, Darlene. I didn't come here to fight with you, and I'm not trying to make you out to be a bad mother. You obviously just need some help."

"I don't need shit from you. Or from Mona Monroe. You can get out of my office now."

Bette stiffens, and her face is blotchy red under her makeup.

She walks right past me. Mom picks up her phone and asks for Nurse Monroe's immediate supervisor. She does not look my way.

I walk a little behind Bette. She turns around to face me after a minute. "Why don't you come stay at my house tonight?"

And then what? I can't stay forever. And I'm too big to fit in a basket and leave myself on someone's doorstep. Even someone as nice as Bette can't adopt me like a kitten she found in a box. And even if she said she could, there wouldn't be room for two.

"I have to stay home, Bette. I have to take care of Andy."

She looks like she might cry. "Show me where you live."

Still hot, still cold. I don't care anymore. At least I can prove I'm not homeless. "Fine."

We walk across the complex, past #80, with the door busted in by the cops more than a week ago. Past #121, where I found my TV/VCR in the closet. Past #60, the one that's mostly burned on the inside.

But #61, second floor above the laundry room, stands alone. "It's that one, up there."

"Show me," she says.

She follows me up the stairs, her heels clicking against the stones embedded in the concrete.

"This is it." I gesture over my shoulder at the closed door.

"Can I come in?"

"Not really," I tell her.

Just take me away. I'll change my name.

"Why not?"

"The door is broken," I explain.

I turn and boost myself over the busted AC unit and work my fingers into the gap in the window. I shove it open and pull myself through. I stand up and part the blinds with my hands, looking out at her.

I can see it when the smell hits her. She puts a hand up to her mouth and looks a little more scared than before.

"Oh, Layla. I had no idea. Why's it so dark in there?"

"Light's broken, too." I can't look at her anymore. "I have to go."

She reaches out and tries to take my hand again. I step back a little.

"Layla, I'm going to get you out of there. You and your little brother. This is not okay."

I've heard this promise before. Social workers are always nice ladies with good clothes who look very concerned and are really convinced they can do something to change the disaster in progress that is my life. And then we move away in the middle of the night, and it all resets.

"Okay." I go to close the window.

She puts her hand in the way. "No, really. Help is on the way." She's actually crying now.

"Okay." I'm pushing her hand out of the slot. I'd chop it off right now if it meant I could close the window and bring this to an end.

I hear her click back down the steps. I slide into my hiding spot and find my camera fully charged. I stay in there until my eyes are dry and I can breathe like a normal human.

Andy comes home and calls my name in the dark house. I don't say anything.

I can't show anybody the video I made. The shark I saw in my mother's eyes today makes that clear. I don't know how she could make things worse, but she always finds a way. She always talks her way around those clipboard ladies, always threatens to get the school nurse fired. She'll get rid of Bette, too. Somehow. I am not a real scientist. I am not proving anything. I am still the kid in the bath with the knife. My experiments always fail.

Sunday 9:30 a.m.

I go to the stupid park. I film the stupid bees in the stupid honeysuckle. I find stupid regular mushrooms and a stupid white moth. I film stupid squirrels and stupid birds. *Otospermophilus beecheyi* and *Passer domesticus.* Stuff anybody could have found. I narrate the whole stupid thing. It's done.

I have to go to the stupid school and use their stupid computers to edit this stupid video. But I can't do that until tomorrow.

And now there's nothing to do and nowhere to go but home.

Nobody's there.

I've undertaken cleaning up the house before. It works best if nobody's home. If Mom says one word to me about it, I quit on the spot. And Andy is helpless. But I should expect trouble, after yesterday. So I return to the processes that have worked in the past.

The dishwasher is full of bugs, and the last load that was put in it is still dirty.

Everything stuck to the plates is dry. I empty out the sink and boil a few pots of water to pour in and get washing.

The dishes take two hours, but at least there's soap. After that, I start throwing away the boxes of Hamburger Helper. They're beyond done. Most of the cardboard has been chewed along the bottom, and macaroni spills out everywhere when I try to pick up a box.

After a while, I hear the bucket spilling over in the bathroom and I run cursing at it, going to siphon it out.

The kitchen's not really clean. I can't get any of the sticky stuff off the counter or mop the floor. There's still mold on the walls, and the fridge is still a biohazard. But it's better. I open the kitchen window to let it air out.

After that, I start pulling up wet newspaper. It comes up in thick layers that tear apart like soggy bread. The smell that comes from underneath it is like rotten eggs and mold. I can barely stand it. I pull up as much as I can and then realize the trash bag is too heavy to lift. I heave it out the window and it lands with a splat on the parking lot below, not far from the dumpster. I'll go get it later.

I put down fresh paper and work on the general living-room crap. I find more mushrooms growing out of a pair of Andy's old swim shorts in a corner. I throw away the shopping bag from the mall, and it only hurts for a second before I shove it out of my mind.

It's looking better here than it has in months. Not enough that Mom would let maintenance in to fix the sink. Or the door. But I'm not even sure that's possible anymore. I can see the wood of the frame warping at the bottom, where it's always wet.

That door might never open again.

I may have cleaned up enough so that she'll notice, but there's nothing she can say to me about it that would sound good. It's still not enough to head off trouble, if Bette comes back with help.

Not enough that I could let anyone in. Still. I find a can of soup that's only a little past its expiration date. No dents. I set it aside to make for Andy's dinner.

5:00 p.m.

Mom and Andy come home, and I don't even ask. And she doesn't say anything. And nothing changes.

My phone vibrates and it's Kristi.

Hey, did you do the project?

I did *my* project.

-_- I didn't have any time to film mine. My mom has been freaking out at me.

Ok

Can I please help you edit yours and we can call it a group thing?

I sit and stare at my phone for a bit. There is no universe where it's fair for Kristi to ask me for anything.

I guess. But it better be super fancy editing.

I'll bring my laptop tomorrow.

Fine.

I make Andy bring me his backpack. He whines about each assignment, but we get it all done. He reads to me from his book, and I correct him when the words are hard and he messes them up.

"Is sluggish the language that slugs speak?" he asks me, his lisp terrible on every word.

"No, it means to go really slow. Like a slug goes."

"It sounds like a language."

The linguistics of Pulmonata. It's a funny idea, but I don't laugh.

"I know. Keep going."

We keep going.

Monday 1:15 p.m.

Raleigh gives us half the period to work on our projects. I pop out the memory card, and Kristi puts it into her MacBook.

She pulls up the files and looks at them.

"What are these first ones? The thumbnails are all dark." She's squinting at her screen.

"Nothing. Mistakes. Delete those and just use the second folder."

She opens the footage of the park, and her pink lips scrunch all the way over to one side.

"This stuff is okay. All the plants are out of focus, though. You need to not be so close to them."

"Well, I never did it before!" I hover over her, trying to see how she does all this.

"It's not your fault. We can reshoot it today, on the way home. Do you want to come over?"

"I can't."

She keeps fiddling while she talks to me. "My mom said you might be weird about it. She says to tell you to come anyway. She's making your favorite dinner."

"What's my favorite dinner?"

"She asked me what your favorite was, so I told her it was fried chicken. Sorry, Layla. I didn't know the answer, so I took a shot. Anyway, you have to come. She's like obsessed with you right now."

Is that jealousy? I'd be jealous, I think.

"Fine, we'll shoot on the way over."

When she ejects the drive, I can tell she deleted the files of my house.

For a minute I wonder if the original files are still on the SD card.

5:15 p.m.

Kristi shows me how to get really good details up close on the flowers. She says she'll show me some of how the editing program works on her computer, before dinner.

We're working at her kitchen table when her mom shows up.

"Hi, girls. How was your day?"

"Fine." We say it at the exact same time.

"Did anything good happen today?" She's pretending to talk to both of us, but she's only looking at me.

"We got all the filming for our project finished."

"That's great! Anything else?"

I look at Kristi, who shrugs. "Not really. Why?"

Bette's face falls a little. "Did anybody come and talk to you today?"

"Like who?" I'm watching her very carefully.

"Nobody, I guess. Just . . . wanting to hear something out of the ordinary. I'm going to start dinner."

We escape the table and go up to Kristi's room. She's working on more poems.

"Here, how about this?"

She takes her special poet stance and uses her special poet voice.

"Tragic whispers
Lie to keep us apart
But no one knows the truth
That I keep in my heart."

"Is this about that Twitter thing?"

She drops her arms. "Yes, it's about that Twitter thing. Now listen!"

"Fine, fine."

"Just waiting for the clock
To strike the thirteenth hour of never
Because only on the keyboard
Are U and I together."

"Oh my god."

"What?" She looks anxious.

"I . . . I never noticed that those two letters are right next to each other."

Kristi smiles. "Here, I want to show you something." She pulls a notebook out of her bag and flips the pages for a minute. "Look."

On the page is a short black-and-white comic strip starring Emerson Berkeley. He's riding in the boat on the River Styx behind Death, looking bored. As they round the corner, Emerson looks up and says to Death, "Isn't it a little bright in here?"

I laugh out loud at it.

Kristi smiles. "You were right. He really does like my drawings. And Sean . . . he's not my dad, but he was actually really cool to me when my mom was being all weird."

I smile back at her. "That's great! You should tweet this at Emerson."

"Oh, no way. Mackenzie and that bitch Jane will never shut up about it. Just when I think I have them blocked, they pop up out of nowhere."

"Hey . . . um, that reminds me. Were they planning some kind of prank on me?"

Kristi puts her notebook down slowly. "How did you find out about that?"

"Just rumors," I lie. "How did you?"

She picks up her laptop off the floor. "You seriously need to be on Twitter. I know you can't do it on your phone, but you can tweet from a computer. And people talk about you on there. A lot."

"I can do it on my phone if I have Wi-Fi," I mumble. I check to see if I'm connected to her home network. I'm not, so Kristi gives me the password.

Fifteen minutes later, I have an account and a picture that Kristi took with her iPhone.

"Jane is @angelface787. Mackenzie is @macktheknife and Ryan Audubon is @ryguyshyguy." She clicks on all of them fast to set my account to follow them, and then scrolls back down their timelines to find the prank plans.

"Here it is. From last week. God, Mackenzie tweets so many pics."

@macktheknife: that wouldn't even embarrass her

@ryguyshyguy: a whole Instagram just for pics of her? idk that seems pretty embarrassing

@angelface787: I sit right behind her in second period, I have sooo many pics of her hair

@angelface787: it's so fuckin gross I should get paid for smelling it

@angelface787: so not fair to me

@macktheknife: yeah but it's not like she'll see it. She
     doesn't even have a smart phone

@angelface787: no but I can hook up my laoptop to
     the projector in honors English and show it to
     everyone

@ryguyshyguy: oh shit

@macktheknife: u r gonna end up getting in trouble
     for bullying

@angelface787: ill put a password on the Instagram

@angelface787: they'll never fucking catch me

@ryguyshyguy: ur cold @angelface787 #bitchesbecold

@angelface787: dilligaf?

I'm not in my body right now. I'm floating five feet above it, and where my body used to be there's just fire.

"I told them to leave you alone." Kristi says it very quietly. "I don't know if they actually made that Instagram. I haven't seen it, and nobody has mentioned it since then."

"What's dilligaf?"

"It's 'Does it look like I give a fuck?' It's an anagram."

It's an acronym. I open up my newly made Twitter account and write my first tweet.

@airyoddknee: I guess this is how it is now.
     #bitchesbecold

Somehow this conversation I've never seen before is worse than the ones that involve someone with perfect teeth sneering in my face. I don't follow their accounts, but I make a list of their @ names. #lurker.

I am not going to school tomorrow.

Tuesday 6:30 a.m.

I have to be at school today—it's my day on shift in the kitchen.

I lay out frozen hash browns on the big silver tray and slide them into the oven. When they come out, I eat one too fast and burn the roof of my mouth. That's life.

Kristi gave me the camera back, and I was thinking of trying to film part of breakfast this morning. I wish I'd had the camera the day that girl passed out. But who knows what today will bring?

I'm not on the serving line today, which means once everything is cooked I can get out of my plastic apron and hairnet. In the back of the kitchen, I stand up near the ovens, scarfing down slice after slice of warm ham. I get two whole cartons of orange juice, and it already feels like it's going to be a great day.

In second period, I take my usual seat. I sit completely still and wait until I'm sure I hear Jane's phone taking pictures behind me.

I turn to face her.

"What the hell are you doing?"

She rolls her eyes. "Nothing."

"Jane, why are you taking pictures of me?" I let my voice rise until it's practically hysterical. "Why, Jane? Why would you do that? It's so weird! Why?"

She starts to look alarmed just as Ms. Valenti walks over, tall in her black suit and as crisp as ever.

"What's all this disruption about? Jane? Are you taking photos of Layla without her consent?"

Jane's eyes narrow and she gives me the look of death. "No. She's lying and being a spaz, like usual."

I can barely keep from laughing. I try to channel it into hysteria. "She did! It's true, she did! She does it all the time! Look at her phone, Ms. Valenti. You'll see. She's always bullying me. Sometimes . . . sometimes I think I should just die."

At the end of the sentence, my voice breaks because I am going to laugh myself to death. I put my head on my arms on top of my desk and try to make it sound like sobbing. A few years ago, like fourth grade, these sobs would be real. I've learned a lot since then.

"Let's see your phone, Jane." Valenti is holding out her hand, palm up.

"You're not allowed to take my phone. It's my property."

Valenti sighs, and her thin lips get thinner. "You're right about that. So how about you pull up your gallery and show me the last photo you took?"

They stare at each other a minute. Valenti drops her voice. "Jane. You've been warned about this before. You need to come talk to me after class."

Jane holds up her phone and shows Valenti something I can't see.

"Delete that. And if I catch you doing it again, I will not let it slide."

Ms. Valenti walks away, and I straighten up in my chair.

Jane hisses in my ear. "Doesn't matter. I have lots more."

Of course she does. And I guess it doesn't matter. But it still feels like a great day.

12:15 p.m.

It's still a great day when I tell Kristi what happened at lunch. Kristi's bento is simpler today, mostly fruit and vegetables. I guess she and her mom are doing better.

I'm halfway through the plasticky cheese pizza, watching Kristi read over Jane's timeline from this morning, when today completely goes to hell.

"Okay, around second period, she tweeted, 'snitches get stitches lol.' And then, like an hour later—"

"Layla!"

I inhale so sharply that the bite of pizza almost gets sucked into my windpipe. I choke it out onto the plate, my eyes watering. There is no way.

"Layla!"

I stand up and turn around slow, like in a nightmare. It's Mom. She's wearing the leggings that are see-through over her ass, and her shirt could not possibly be more wrinkled. Her eyes are wide and wild and she's coming right at me.

What can I kill myself with? Even the forks are plastic.

"Layla, are you wearing my jeans?"

"What?"

Her hands are on me, and the shock is so complete that I can't even move. I stand there like a mannequin while she beats at my pockets.

"Are these my jeans? Did you take my jeans this morning?"

I don't say anything. She grabs both of my shoulders and shakes me a little.

"No. These are my jeans. I just got them."

She looks down for a second, like she's not really hearing me. There is not a single sound in the lunchroom. I can hear every rattle in her throat when she breathes, and I know she woke up hacking and headed here before she really got the morning cough out of her system. She reeks of old cigarettes and piss and the perfume she tries to spray over that smell. I stumble backward to get her hands off me and end up sitting down hard on the bench again.

They're all looking at me. Well, not all of them. Feels like all of them, but a lot of them are looking at their phones, or at each other.

Too many are looking at me. I can't believe they're not staring at her. Too afraid to, I guess. Maybe she's what they're laughing at, the ones who are laughing. Maybe they're just laughing out of relief that it's not happening to them. She's the one who deserves their staring, but they know me. They *think* they know me.

I glance back at Mom and she's only kind of looking at me. It's like she's afraid to make eye contact with me; she always seems to talk to the center of my chest or to my shoulder. Like if we gaze into each other's eyes, something terrible will happen.

Something terrible *is* happening. Right now.

She opens up her mouth, and I can see she's folding toilet paper over her bottom teeth again. She started doing that about a year ago. I can't figure out if it's because her teeth hurt or because she can't deal with how black and holey they are, or if even she got tired of the smell.

It doesn't fool anybody. Any idiot can tell toilet paper from teeth. Sometimes when she's yelling, she blows the wet wad of spongy white stuff out onto her lip. Then she just mashes it back in and moves on.

She's doing that right now. She licks her cracked lips and looks scared.

But I think I'm the only one close enough to see that. To smell her. The scientific name for bad breath is *halitosis*. Knowing that gives me no feeling of control.

"Those jeans have four hundred dollars in their pocket. Did you take the money? Did your brother take it?"

Oh god don't go to Andy's school.

"No, Mom. Nobody touched your jeans. Or your money. I need you to go. Right now. Can you go, right now, please?" I'm trying to keep my voice down, but I'm barely winning that fight.

She looks at my pockets again, and I swear to god if she touches me this time I will start screaming, and I will maybe never stop.

She walks away without saying anything else, just walks out of the room as if she didn't just destroy my one small moment of peace, my one good day.

All over the room, there's the sudden sound of phones going off. Kristi's beeps right beside me. Together, we sink down and try to disappear.

"What are they saying?"

Kristi doesn't answer, she just hands me her phone.

@angelface787: wtf was that thing

@ryguyshyguy: well that just happened

@macktheknife: u guys wtf was that im scared???

@angelface787: ok now I get it #likemotherlikedaugh-
ter lmaooooo

Wednesday 11:30 a.m.

I never know when it's going to be my last day. I never really have to say goodbye, but I never really get to, either.

I remember before we moved to California. Andy's too little to remember any of that; he was just a big baby when Dad left. Talking, but still in diapers. Totally useless.

It's hard to remember my last day at my school in Missouri, because I didn't know it was going to be my last. I know that it was the day before winter break. I remember the white snowflakes we cut out and hung on the windows while real snow piled up outside. I remember taking the bus home, with all the kids talking about going to visit their grandmas and their cousins, or else taking off for somewhere warmer.

We were going to take off, too. But not yet.

I don't remember Dad leaving, because at first there wasn't any difference. He was in the Army, and he was never home. And then he was never *coming* home. I guess that matters, but I didn't see how at first.

The important thing was that we used to get money from him and we weren't going to anymore. I heard Mom yelling about it on the phone, over and over. When the phone stopped working, I was glad. Then the lights went out and I was less glad.

Mom stopped leaving the house. The dark windows had frost at the edges, and Andy had to wear his coat inside, all the time. Nobody stopped by to visit. Christmas came and went; I didn't even bother asking. Mom had stopped talking.

I think they're not allowed to shut off your gas when you live somewhere that it snows. There's no way we paid the bill, but the gas stayed on. That meant the water heater and the stove worked.

We ate out of cans for a long time. I remember corn and soup at first, and then cans of pumpkin or beets, or jars of spaghetti sauce we'd just eat with spoons. Andy cut himself trying to use the can opener, and he cried and cried. I wrapped his fingers up and put a sock over his hand. Mom never even looked at it. She stopped looking at us, or at anything.

I slept in Andy's crib with him, with every blanket and towel piled around us, and we still froze. I have nightmares that we're still there, the dark so complete that I can't see him or my own hands, the cold so sharp that I have to cover our faces.

One night we were so cold I thought we would die. I didn't know anything back then; I don't know if it was actually cold enough to kill. The window rattled and whistled in Andy's room, and cold air came through. I didn't know what to do about that either, but before the sun went down I could see our breath inside the house. When my hands and feet were numb, I climbed out and got Andy to follow. We went to the bath.

Back then there weren't even candles. We felt for the drain plug and the faucet; we turned on the water and waited for it to get hot. I climbed into the tub with him and we both stopped shivering. I picked up a bottle of shampoo, but it was frozen solid. We fell asleep in the water, only waking up when our hair dripped cold on us or when we had to warm up the bath again.

When I thought dawn must be coming, I got out of the tub and wrapped a blanket around myself. I wondered how Mom was going to make it through the night all by herself. There was no one on the couch, but I knew right away by the glow.

In the kitchen, the oven was on full blast—I could even see the flames coming up from the broiler. Mom was lying across three dining-room chairs, wrapped in her blankets and snoring.

I didn't have the words for it then, but that was the moment I realized we were enemies. Not just that she didn't like us; that was always obvious. But that she probably flat-out hated us and maybe thought we could die quietly one of these cold nights.

I got Andy dressed again and wrapped blankets around us both. Quietly, I led him to the kitchen and laid him down on the floor in front of the roaring oven. I lay behind him and we slept, warmer than we had been in weeks.

At some point, we had our last night in that house. I don't remember it. We moved here, where it's never cold enough for that to happen again.

Yesterday could have been my last day at my school, but I'd remember it forever.

I still can't believe she came to my school.

It's the first time she's said my name in ages.

And it's the first time she's put her hands on me since we moved to California. Of that, I am deadly sure.

Today, Andy is in school but I'm not. There's no way I was going after what happened yesterday. Mom hasn't been home since then. I'm in my hideout, watching *Auntie Mame*, waiting for Kristi to text me that she's done editing our project.

I've still got the camera. I still like the idea that I might see something cool and capture it. Maybe put it on my Twitter account. Maybe distract people from the Instagram about me—if that really exists. I don't buy it. Jane Chase doesn't have that much time to spend on a prank like that. It isn't even funny.

In the afternoon, I hear Andy come through the window, and I'm about to slide back in and meet him when I hear something else. It's the same sound Andy makes coming through, but confused. Longer. Clumsier. And then it comes again.

"This is your house, Andrew?"

My veins turn to ice. An adult woman, someone I don't know, is in my house. I hit the power button on my TV.

"Yeah, this is it." He has no idea.

"Where is your mommy right now?" An adult man, another stranger.

"She's at work right now."

A million things go quick through my head. Kidnappers, child molesters, those people who sell kids for money. They could be anybody.

No. I know who they are. I just can't deal with it.

"Where is your sister? Where's Layla?" The woman again.

Andy sounds unsure. "I thought she was at school, but then I didn't see her."

The man answers. "We went to her school first to talk to her. She wasn't there."

"Oh. Sorry."

"It's okay, Andrew. Can you show me the kitchen?"

Their voices muffle as they walk to the other side of the apartment. I can tell they're talking but can't make out a word. I pick them back up in the living room.

"Mommy sleeps there." Andy sounds so, so small.

"Your mommy sleeps on the couch?"

"Uh-huh. She doesn't like her room anymore."

"Can you show me her room?" The woman's got a voice like a kindergarten teacher.

They're in the room right next to me now. My hideout is just below her window.

I can hear the woman choking when they walk in. "What happened in here?"

"Mommy used to have a waterbed, but it broke."

There's a little silence, and then I hear one of them say softly, "Water damage . . . rotted the . . . boxes."

Loud again, in that kindergarten-teacher tone. "Andy, can you show me the bathroom?"

He gives them the tour. I hear them asking where the sheets are for his bed, or for my bed. I hear them asking who makes him dinner and where he keeps his clothes.

Andy is completely honest with them, and patient, and sounds like he's trying to get a good grade on a test. Trying so hard. I'm clawing at my jeans, but I don't realize it until I hear the sound I'm making. I wish I could get my hands over his mouth, or he could hear me telling him with my mind to shut up.

They're not kidnappers. They're not here to molest him. They're from CPS and they came to take him away. The clipboard people. I'm holding on to myself with both hands. If I come up now, they'll take us both. But if they just take him, I'll never see him again. I've seen them take kids from our neighbors before.

The woman talks to Andy very sweetly, like she's afraid to scare him. "Andrew, we are going to take you somewhere. It will be somewhere safe and nice, and you'll get to have some dinner there. Will you come with us?"

There's no answer.

"Andrew, will you please come with us? To a safe place?"

He's crying. I can hear his hitching breath and his stupid baby voice. "I want my mommy. We should go to her work, it's not even far! I can walk there!"

"We—we are going to talk to your mommy. Mr. Evans here is going to go see her right now. But I'd like you to come with me while he does that."

"I want my mommy! I want Layla." He stops talking to them and just yells out for me. "Layla! Layla!"

My hands are pressed against my cardboard walls. I'm convinced he knows I'm there. He's calling for me because he knows I can hear him. *Oh god oh god.*

"Layla! Don't let them take me away! Layla! I'm getting tooken away!"

"Can you open this door, Julius?"

"I'm trying. It really won't budge."

"Jesus. Okay, you go through the window and I'll pass him to you."

"Ugh. Alright, hold my jacket, at least."

I can hear them struggling with the window and with Andy. Andy screams and cries, and by the sound of it, he's kicking all the way out the window, too.

"Layla! Layla, don't let them take me! Layla!"

The sound of his screaming fades as they take him down the stairs and away, away, away.

I can't think. I know once he's gone it's all over. *But I can't think I can't think I can't think they took my brother.*

They're going to be back for me.

They already went to my school. They're going to talk to my mom. They're going to find me.

I don't hear another sound in the house until two days later.

Friday 8:00 a.m.

I get shocked awake by the banging and wrenching noises of the front door as it's broken and opened up.

I've snuck out of my hiding space a couple of times, but I'm glad I stayed in today. It sounds like five or six people coming through the front door after breaking it down.

I charged my phone last night and the camera all day yesterday. I packed my backpack the night after they took Andy. I'm ready.

I should have left before dawn. Now I don't know how long these people are going to stay.

I slide out of my cardboard tunnel and peek slowly up over the window into Mom's room. They brought in big standing lights, with cords running out the door. My heart is in my throat for a moment when I realize they're probably plugged in where I am. They might find my cord in the laundry room downstairs and follow it up. Find me.

Someone walks into Mom's room and I slip back down. For a second I can't make sense of what I'm seeing. It doesn't even look like a person.

When I get the courage to look back up, there's a blinding light in the room and now there's two of them.

Two big people. No, not that big. They're just wearing some kind of big plastic suits with respirators. I can hear them talking, some in Spanish and some in English.

"So this is an abandonment, or what?"

"Yeah, the tenant just split, so the place has been vacant for who knows how long. The owner came and looked at it after the cops got a hold of him."

"Man. What a hole."

"Yeah."

They're wearing big gloves as they start to take apart the furniture. They're getting stuff off the floor with a shovel and a rake-like thing.

I'm recording.

When these two walk out of the room, I decide it's time.

I've only climbed over the railing and down the outside wall twice before. Both times I trembled like a leaf and barely made it. This time, my backpack is heavy and I'm already terrified.

I swing one leg over the railing and sit there a minute. It's stupid, anyone can see me, but I just can't get myself to do it.

Today is my last day here. I know that now.

I swing the other leg down and move my foot blindly to find the beam beneath the balcony. When I've got it securely, I bring my hands down to the bottom of the railing and push my feet out. I hang.

This is the hard part. It isn't that far to drop. About my height, I'm pretty sure.

But the last two times I hit the ground like a sack of trash.

I hear voices in the room above again.

I let go.

I guess if I was in sports I would know how to land right. I would drop in a crouch instead of a pile. But I never learned how to land on my feet. My knees go out and I am sprawled on my ass, my hands scraped and my ankles aching.

I have to get up quick. I have to walk like everything is normal. I didn't come from that house. I came from nowhere.

But I know where I'm going.

9:30 a.m.

Kristi showed me a long time ago how she gets out of her room at night. It works just as well to get in. There's a wooden trellis with little roses growing on it that reaches up to the eave under her bedroom window. She never locks it.

Nobody is home. No black Mercedes, no white SUV. Total silence when I hit the floor in Kristi's pink bedroom.

I throw all my clothes in the washer, including the ones I have on. I put on a robe I find in the dryer.

In the kitchen, I make myself a cup of tea and warm up some leftovers I find in the fridge. I sit at their table, in their silence, and I steal their life.

It's okay, they'll never miss it.

They will never miss these twenty minutes of silence and peace. They have so much clean order they'll never know any of it is missing.

I eat it all. The food, the light, the chair, the table. I eat Kristi's safety and her mom's love. I eat her stepdad's job and her sister's fancy college tuition. I'm stuffed with it when I put my clothes in the dryer. I eat like I'm never going to eat again.

Because I probably won't.

I take a long shower, this time in Bette's bathroom. I brush my hair all the way out, using her fancy conditioner and special comb. I shave my legs and armpits with her razor. I use her deodorant.

I get dressed and roll the rest of my clothes into tight cylinders, fit them in around books in my bag. Looking in my backpack, I think about the fact that I have no money. Not a cent. Nothing I can really sell.

I can sleep in my secret RV until I get caught or scared away. I know some places I can hide, and I can always find more. I will need money someday. I have no idea what I'll do about that.

I'm dressed. I'm ready. I'm sitting in Kristi's room, and I can't make myself leave yet. Not yet. Not without a better plan than running to nowhere.

I think of Mom in the cafeteria the other day, and I wonder if that is the last time I will see her. I don't even know how I feel about that.

I stopped wondering a long time ago why some people have lives like Kristi's while I have this one. I don't think there are any rules on that. It's just what we get.

But today I'm wondering if there's anything I can do to change that. Today I am thinking about that stupid little girl in the bathtub who finally just brushed her own damn hair.

It's still wet from the shower. Sitting up, I can see myself in Kristi's mirror. I'm clean. I'm dressed in clean clothes. My mom is gone, and nobody carried me off kicking and screaming. I did this. That's worth something.

Kristi's laptop is on the floor again. I slide the SD card into the slot.

Editing the video takes longer than I thought. The program is simple once I know where the tools are, but finding them takes forever the first time. I'm watching the clock. I turn my phone on and it's full of messages from Kristi and Bette and numbers I don't recognize. All of a sudden everyone's looking for me.

My Twitter account has a bunch of new mentions and DMs. There's even a couple of nice ones, people asking if I'm alright or if I need help. I could spend the time replying to everybody one by one. Or I could just say this once and then drop the mic.

Once the video is ready, I get into Kristi's makeup bag. I don't know what I'm doing at all, but I screw with it until I can at least put on mascara and eyeliner. I want people to be able to see my eyes. I sit on Kristi's big pink bed and flip on her webcam.

"My name is Layla Bailey, and this is my biome."

I cut to the footage of my house, turning up the audio so that I can be heard explaining my habitat. I added today's men in plastic suits to the very end, and I narrate over it.

"These people and CPS are the apex predators of my ecosystem, and I am an endangered species. The last of my kind. But the Sierra Club doesn't make posters out of kids like me."

I add three screenshots near the end. The first is the only picture of my mom I could find, in profile and wreathed in smoke.

"This is my mother, Darlene Thompson. She was born in captivity and released into the wild without any skills to care for herself. She is missing. If you see her, do not attempt to approach her, but please contact animal control."

The second is of Andy.

"This is Andrew Fisher Bailey, my little brother. He was taken into captivity two days ago by people he had never seen before. I don't know his whereabouts, but I hope he's safe. If you see him, remember he is friendly but skittish. He is better off in captivity than in the wild."

The last one is my most recent report card, accessed on the school website by inputting the username and password I created for my mom last year.

"This is me, Layla Louise Bailey. I was born in the wild and cannot be domesticated. However, I'm not yet fully capable of caring for myself, either. I have no money and not enough skills. What I have is a 4.0 and really low standards. I'll do chores. I'll be quiet. If you've got a garage or a laundry room I could sleep in, I am mostly housebroken. I just want to finish school, adopt my little brother, and go to college."

I type my phone number, email, and Twitter handle over a still frame of the mushrooms I filmed in Andy's dresser. I don't know how long my phone will work, but I can use the computers at the library to check email and Twitter. They can contact me, but not find me. Unlike Andy, I'm free.

It turns out Jane Chase's Instagram isn't just about me. I'm on there, mostly close-up pictures of my hair or my clothes with a tag cloud underneath them that I can barely stand to read. There are also pics of a girl with scars from cutting herself, a teacher from our school who has a really bad stutter, and a girl who just started dressing like a girl this year. It's kind of comforting to know Jane's mean to everyone.

The best thing is that anyone can comment and she has a huge number of followers. I'm hoping it's mostly people from our school. That could really help.

The worst feeling here is that I'm not the scientist. I'm the subject. Jane's observations on her Instagram and Bette's decisions about my habitat will determine my fate. Someone else will get to name me and define me. I don't want their pity, and I can't stand the way life just keeps happening to me and I have no control. I am not an experiment. I'm not one of the chimps. I'm Dr. Jane fucking Goodall. And this is the only way I can prove it.

I upload the video and copy and paste the tag cloud she usually puts on stuff about me. Then I tweet the video off of YouTube and tag Jane, Mackenzie, Kristi, Ryan, Amber, and the school's official Twitter account until I hit the character limit.

It's time to leave. I shut down Kristi's Mac and set it on her dressing table instead of the floor. I write her a short thank-you note on her pretty pink paper and leave it next to her computer. I ask her to thank her mom for me, too.

I walk down the stairs slowly. I hope that I'll find somewhere to live so that I can keep going to the same school, and maybe keep Kristi as my best friend. I still don't know why we're best friends, but I'd rather have her than nobody.

But like I said, it's hard to know when it's my last day. So I take a final look around. I've always loved this place. Even if it wasn't mine to love.

When I'm done doing that, I head for the door. Just as I'm about to leave, Bette walks in.

2:00 p.m.

She looks shocked, but I don't blame her. She puts down her grocery bags and comes toward me with her hands out.

"Layla! Where have you been? People are looking for you! How did you get in here?" Her plucked eyebrows are coming together and she's reaching for my hands. I sidestep her a little.

"Hi, Bette. I'm sorry, I let myself in. I just needed to borrow something from Kristi. I'm leaving right now. I'm sorry."

She steps back to block me from going out the door.

"No, Layla. It's okay, you're allowed in this house anytime. But you can't leave. I can't let you."

"Why not?"

"Layla." She swallows and looks around a little. "Layla, where have you been? CPS came to your house and didn't find you. They took your brother into foster care. They're still looking for you . . . and for your mother. Do you know where she might be? Did you leave home with her?"

"No."

"Come sit down. Come talk to me. Will you please do that?"

I'm watching her pretty carefully. "You can't call anyone. I'm not getting taken away like Andy did."

"Honey, these people are trying to do what's right for you. They want to help."

"I mean it. Don't call. Don't touch your phone." I try to tell her with my tone that I'm not kidding.

She stares me down. "Fine. Come sit for a minute, at least."

I sit on the sofa across from her favorite chair, where I know she'll sit.

"Layla. I knew you were in trouble, but I didn't realize how bad it was. I'm sorry. I should have found a way to help sooner."

"Okay." I'm looking at the arm of her chair, to the side of her hand. I don't have to look at anything.

"Your mother . . . I don't even know what to say. I just always assumed she was a busy woman. But your grades were so good I thought she must have done something right."

"I do my own schoolwork. My grades have nothing to do with her." Amazing how much fire there is in that one assumption. That she should get any kind of credit.

"That's not really how it works, honey. Kids . . . most students perform based on the kind of support they receive at home. In a way, it would have been better if you were doing poorly. Then someone might have known before now."

"Sorry to disappoint." The venomous octopus is with me again, arms wrapping around my throat from the inside, where no one can see. But I'm sure Bette can hear it. I'm strangling.

"That's not what . . . look. I don't know what's going to happen. I don't know where you're going to go. Is there any chance your father . . . ? Where is he? I've never heard you mention him." I haven't even thought about my dad in years. Couldn't picture his face if I tried.

"I don't have to go to a foster home. Not if I can make a deal with somebody."

"What?"

"I can take care of myself. Earn my keep somewhere."

Her voice goes from gentle to patronizing. "Sweetie, you're fourteen. That's not how it works."

"Almost fifteen."

"Even so. You're still a minor. CPS will have to find a place for you." Quick glance at her face and there it is: concern like always, but something else underneath. Pity.

I don't want any of that. Not even a little bit. I'd rather live in a box.

Bette is trying to say something, but her phone is ringing. She frowns at it before picking up.

"Kristi? Why are you calling me during class? Are you okay?"

She's silent for a minute, but her eyes rise to mine.

"What video?" It's not just confusion in her voice. It's something like panic. What did Kristi tell her?

I get up and walk to the door. Feels like I'm moving very slowly, like in a nightmare where you can't run.

"Layla! Layla, wait."

I look back and realize she can't actually stop me. She won't handcuff me to her nice furniture. She won't physically hold me down. I can just walk out of here.

So I wave goodbye to her while she talks into her phone, and I go straight through the door.

Midnight

I wish there were more blankets in this RV.

I walked to the school and labeled all of my homework for each teacher, with a note that said to put it in their boxes. The school was all locked down, but I stuck it behind the bars that cover the registrar's window. They'll see it when they open on Monday, plus they won't know when I was there. I folded it in half and stuck it tight between the bars and the glass. Then I found some rocks and carefully weighted it down. It should still be there when they open.

Walking back was so cold. It hardly ever rains here, and there's no wind at all tonight. Just a perfectly crisp, cold, clear night with a tiny sliver of a moon. I'm wearing two shirts, but I don't have a coat. Not even a hoodie. I pull my arms inside my shirts, but that makes my backpack start to slip. I trade off arms the whole walk back, but I'm shaking by the time I get inside.

There's nothing useful in this RV. Boxes of old magazines and junk car parts. Just the one blanket, and it's pretty thin. I pull all my clothes out of my bag and lay them on top of the blanket. It helps a little.

I finally just have to shut my phone off. It vibrated without stopping for almost two hours after I walked out on Bette. I figured she might try to follow me in her car, so I ended up jumping the fences in her neighborhood to head toward the crappier parts of town.

Some of the calls were from Kristi and Bette, but lots weren't. I started seeing LA area codes and others I couldn't even place. I'd wanted someone to respond to my video, but I didn't plan how I would deal with it if they did. I watched the little green screen, trying to figure out what to say.

Nothing came to me.

It's quiet over here. The lights are off in the house that this RV belongs to, and even the street light is burned out. It's safe and dark, and all I have to do is figure out how I'm going to eat.

Saturday Morning

I slept past dawn, and I can't figure out what time it is. I wanted to get started earlier, but whatever.

Nobody's outside. The whole block is quiet. After I've slipped out, I can see kids watching cartoons through their closed windows. Saturday seems like the best day to do this.

It's only a few minutes' walk back home, but it seems to take forever. I avoid the main roads, and I keep looking over my shoulder. I'm sure no one is following me. But still.

Mom's office has had the same lock code since her very first day. She sent me over dozens of times, to get something she forgot or to check something for her.

The chair is empty, but it feels like she's there. As I sit down, I wobble the glass ashtray and a few butts overflow onto the desktop. Jiggle the mouse and her computer wakes up, tabs still open.

She looked at a lot of ways to get out of town. There are tabs open looking at trains and buses and a couple of posts from people looking to share a ride.

Her email is still open. There are two emails from CPS. One looks like a form letter, but the other one seems like it came from a real person. It doesn't tell me anything new, though.

I dial into her office voicemail and listen to two complaints about broken mailboxes and one person looking for an apartment. Then the calls from CPS start.

"Ms. Thompson, this is Anne Cox with Child Protective Services. Please give me a call . . ." She rattles off a phone number and that's that.

"Ms. Thompson, this is Julius Evans with Child Protective Services. I'm here at Brookhurst Junior High, attempting to interview your daughter . . . uh . . . Layla. They've informed me she did not attend class today. I'd like to speak with both of you. Please call me back at . . ."

I wonder who he talked to at my school. Raleigh? That old-lady registrar who always yells at me when I've been absent?

"Mrs. Bailey—Ms. Thompson, I mean, this is Mona Monroe at Maxfield Elementary. Your son, Andrew, has just been signed out by two officers of the court who are attempting to reach you. Please call me at . . ."

"Darlene, this is Bette. I know that today has probably been pretty hard, but please try to understand that we're all trying to help you. And your kids. Okay? Just let us help you. Okay. Bye."

The next voice is deep, almost booming. "Mrs. Bailey, this is Officer Benson with the Anaheim Police Department . . ."

The hair stands up on the back of my neck. A real actual cop.

"Please contact me regarding your appearance in court."

His number follows. Holy shit.

"Ms. Thompson, this is Anne Cox again, calling regarding your son, Andrew. He's been placed in emergency foster care until your hearing on Monday. You are entitled to visitation with him. Please contact me for the information on where he is and how to proceed."

I open tabs for Facebook, my email, and Twitter. I don't log in. I think.

If I called and pretended to be Mom, they would tell me where Andy was. I couldn't show up there, or I'd get busted. I would know where he was, but it wouldn't matter. I could find out when the hearing was, but I couldn't show up to that, either. They might be able to tell that the call came from this office, and then I couldn't ever come back here.

I start logging in to my stuff, but I'm overwhelmed on every page. I have hundreds of DMs on Twitter, and thousands of mentions. I've gained nearly two thousand followers. I can't make sense of what I'm seeing. My ears are ringing.

I have over a hundred new emails. I see some from teachers, from Kristi and other kids I know. I have emails from people I've never met.

I have Facebook friend requests from reporters. I have messages from people I don't know, and I've been tagged in hundreds of posts and photos. I hear a sound in my ears like there are beehives in my head. I tap one of these tags at random and see that it's my video.

But it was posted by some local news team.

I find it again, posted by Elite Daily. And BuzzFeed. And ViralNova. It's everywhere.

On Twitter, there are links to Jane Chase's Instagram, and pictures of my face photoshopped onto "wanted" posters and milk cartons. My hands shake so bad that Google has to guess that I meant YouTube and not "youoyutubrube."

The exact number of views on my biome video is 602,124. That number feels impossible, made up. If everyone I'd ever met had watched it, it still wouldn't be this many.

I slip out of the chair and under the desk. I press myself into the little cubicle underneath the wooden top. This seems like a good place.

I can't breathe right, and I decide I'm going to stay down here for a while. Nobody can see me, and the electronic lock is still on. I should be safe.

I'm never going to be safe again.

I think about people I know watching this video. I think about Bette and Raleigh and Valenti and their terrible pity. I think of Ryan Audubon laughing, and Amber Rodin tweeting it to her friends. It feels like that dream where I go to school naked, except I'm naked forever on the internet and I can't wake up.

I thought this would make me the scientist. I should have known that the thing that slides out of the petri dish never gets to speak for itself. I know there's no happy ending, but I thought maybe this video could bring me better results. However, I'd have needed a stronger hypothesis. And I didn't know what I was doing, or really why. I just had to do it.

And maybe it will still yield a meaningful finding, but before that I have to live through this feeling of being the thing under the microscope and everybody taking a look, saying my Latin name, guessing at my taxonomy.

I need to hide. I need to answer some of these messages. No, I shouldn't answer anybody. I wonder how hard it would be to pass as Mom on the phone.

Someone is hitting buttons on the door keypad.

The bees are loud. They might be wasps. *Apis mellifera. Pepsis grossa.* I don't know. They both sting. I'm sweating and it's not even hot. I hold my breath and pull my knees up under my chin.

Whoever it is, they're riffling through papers on the desk over my head. I want to shut my eyes but I can't. I see feet come around to behind the desk. It's Mom.

"Where the hell is it?"

If she sees what's on her computer screen, the world will just explode. I'll burst into flames. I'll drop dead. Or she will. Or everyone will.

I mash the glowing button on the surge protector with one sweaty palm.

There's a minute of silence so deep I could drown in it. With everything shut off, not even the hum of the running electronics separates us. It's *H. sapiens* and the silence.

We're in this tiny room together, smaller than the bedroom I used to share with Andy. There's only one way out. Whatever she's going to say, I'll hear it. She could just speak.

She could just say goodbye.

There's the sound of paper one more time and the muffled noise of something being pushed into her pocket. Then the door opens again and she's standing there, waiting.

"Mom?"

I hear something. A sigh, maybe.

She heard me.

I'm like a shaken soda with the cap blown off. What bubbles out of me when she's gone isn't like being angry or ashamed or any of the hot terrible things I've kept crammed inside me for as long as I can remember. It's as sharp and as solid as a scorpion stinger—and even with the way I feel right now, I can still remember its name, it's *Leiurus quinquestriatus*—and the sound of the pain it causes comes out of me like a scream, like when a whistle blows loud and high right in your ear, like the screech of a big owl swooping through the night.

It goes on for a long time. When it's over, I'm empty and tired. I wish she had watched the video and the world had died. I wish a scorpion had stung me for real. I wish I had something to show people, like here's the scar where my mom used to be.

I have nothing. That's life.

I play back the voicemail again, and I call the number for Anne Cox. I am going to get my brother.

Saturday Afternoon

I hang up on Ms. Cox's voicemail. That was never going to work.

I dial the number for Officer Benson, and he picks right up.

"This is Benson."

"Hi, Officer Benson. My name is Amber, and I'm doing a school project on Child Protective Services."

There's a little silence before he answers. "Okay, hi, Amber. How did you get my number?"

"My dad works at the courthouse, and he gave me your card."

"Oh . . . okay. Okay. I only have a minute. Can I answer a quick question for you?"

He can hear me smiling. Everybody says you can hear that over the phone. So I smile real big. "Where does a kid go once CPS takes them away? Is there like an office or what?"

He clears his throat a little. I haven't really put him at ease. "Well, that depends on the age of the child. Older kids generally go to one of the big group homes, but little kids go into temporary foster care until we can get them back home."

"Back home?"

"Yeah, the aim of CPS is always to place children back into their own homes, once the issues have been resolved."

Something about the way he says this sounds like he's said it a thousand times, like the way you rush through a poem you memorized for class.

"What if they can't be resolved?" Keep smiling.

He hesitates. "Then they go into more permanent homes, or even go up for adoption. Listen, Amanda, all of this information is online, you can just—"

"It's Amber, actually." Is he trying to catch me in a lie? "Do you know what happened to Andrew Bailey?"

Longer silence this time. "Why are you asking about him? Do you know him?"

"I know his sister, Layla."

No hesitation at all. "Do you know where she is right now?"

"No, I don't . . . Listen, I was making up the school project thing. A bunch of us just want to send Andy a card so he's not so scared. I just want to find out how we can get it to him." I bite my lip like I'm actually ashamed of the lie.

"I can't tell you that, kiddo. But I tell you what, why don't you bring your card to the police station, and I'll make sure he gets it? Just ask for me at the front desk. Okay?"

"Okay. Thank you, Officer Benson."

"That's alright. Do you think you'll come today?" He is trying to catch me. He's all friendly now, too friendly.

"I don't know, I have to ask my mom for a ride." *Careful. Careful. How would a normal kid talk?*

"You do that. I'll be here until five."

"Thank you. Okay. Bye."

It's a trap. It's obviously a trap. If I show up, he'll know my face. I'd get taken and I'd probably never get a note to Andy.

Foster parents. Adoption. The first stage of mitosis where one cell splits into two, and there's no going back. Interphase, prophase, metaphase, anaphase, telophase, and then there are two. There's no family in the world that would take us both. He's little, though. Cute, even with his broken front tooth. Somebody could adopt him.

He'd be safe. Someone would make sure he got fed and put clothes on him. He'd be better off, really.

But who's going to sit with him on Sunday nights and make him read? How is he going to sleep alone when he has nightmares? He's always had me, since he was a baby and I started changing his diapers when Mom would forget.

I can still hear him yelling my name as they took him away.

I start the computer back up just so that I can sign out of everything. Before I close the window, I see that my video has been watched hundreds of times since I got here.

That's when I figure out what my hypothesis should have been. What I should have been working for.

Saturday Night

Safe in my RV, I start planning my way out. My revenge. My best outcome.

I know how to ride the bus for free. It's a trick I've pulled before: we have a presentation in school about safe places where you can go if you're in trouble and they'll take you in. They have these stickers that look like a big grown-up puffy thing hugging a smaller puffy thing. All the buses have one.

So I tested my hypothesis one day when I needed to go to a different library than the one near my house. The doors with the puffy-people sticker opened, and I got on the bottom step. I looked up at the driver from there, trying to appear and sound younger than I was.

"I'm sorry. I don't have any money, but this weird guy in a long coat was following me. I just need to get away. Is it okay if I just ride for a little while so I can call my mom from somewhere safe?"

The driver was a big man in a crisp light-blue shirt. "Sure thing, girly girl. Get on back there." He smiled at me, and I smiled back. He radioed to somebody about me and my mythical creeper. I rode for four miles and waved to him as I got off. A couple hours later, I pulled the same act on an old-lady driver with long purple fingernails. She looked so worried, scanning the front of the library for my imaginary predator, that I almost felt bad about lying.

So I can use the safe-place mentality of nice people to ride to the police station. I'll drop off my note for Andy at the front desk and leave quickly before anyone can spot me.

Just thinking about Andy hurts right now. At night I can't help but think about him. It's weird to sleep without the little noises he makes, or the accidental knocking of our knees. I wonder who's taking care of him, who's making sure he does his homework. I think about his broken front tooth and his freaky vampire grin. He looked normal before that happened. His hair is straight, and I cut it short every month with an electric clipper thing. He could get adopted. That tooth, though . . .

Here's how Andy got a broken tooth. Nighttime was usually quiet with Mom. Andy and me in my loft bed, Mom either on the couch or out somewhere. If she woke us up in the middle of the night, I knew we were in for something terrible.

That night, she woke us up yelling. I don't remember the words, just the volume and sitting bolt upright in bed, Andy waking up slower.

I remember blinking in the darkness of our room and seeing the light on in the hallway. I sat there for a second, trying to figure out what I had heard.

"*Get up.* Get the wet vac."

Mom was in her bedroom. As soon as I came down the one step into her room, I felt the water on the floor. It was at least an inch high, and this was before the leak in the bathroom, before the layer of newspapers was added to the carpet. I ran down the hallway and Andy followed me.

The wet vac was in the hallway closet, buried under a couple of boxes of junk. She'd bought it at a garage sale after the last time her bed leaked. Waterbeds are the worst invention of all time.

I set the boxes down in the water without thinking that they'd be ruined, and I dragged the vacuum out. I walked into Mom's room and Andy was standing there, watching water pour out of the big plastic bag inside of her waterbed. The blankets were all balled up under the headboard, but they were already soaked. The water just kept coming and coming. I couldn't see from exactly where.

Mom grabbed the cord out of my hand and plugged it in. "Get that thing running before we flood the whole house."

"Do I put the hose on the bed or—"

"On the floor."

Not sure if I was asleep or awake, but I did as I was told. I put the weird trapezoidal head of the vacuum into the water at my feet and flipped on the toggle switch. The vac filled up quickly, chugging too loud to talk. Mom hunted all over the bed to find the hole, tossing stuff out of her way. One side of her bed was covered in books and balled-up tissues and Styrofoam takeout containers and all kinds of junk. Most of it tumbled to the floor and floated there, in the rising water.

I started dragging the full vacuum tank to the sliding glass door at the back of Mom's bedroom. I slid it open and the water poured out onto the balcony on that side. I opened the tank and poured gray water until there was only silt left in there. I closed the machine back up and dragged it back in.

"Close the door."

"But the water's draining out—"

"Somebody will see! Close it." She was still staring at the bed. Her eyes were in deep shadow, and she was chewing her lip. She was already on her way out of herself, I could tell.

I came back around the bed and saw it. I think we saw it at the same time. On the far side of the bed, near where she slept, there was the hole. It was small and low, so that the water had filled up the frame before overflowing from all sides. The hole was round and looked melted.

Cigarette burn. If she had had a regular bed, she'd have set it on fire.

I was very awake at that moment. And very pissed off. I was pissed off that I had to shut the door so that I could run that vacuum all night long. I was pissed off at the way she was staring at the hole, doing nothing, sliding out of reality to leave me to deal with this. Like always.

"Andy, go back to bed." I always have to be in charge. Always.

He looked up at me with fear in his eyes.

"There's nothing for you to do, and you're just in the way. Go back to bed."

He looked at Mom. She stared at the hole.

"Now."

He turned around and left, his little feet splashing in the cold water. I turned the vacuum back on.

I didn't have to watch it; the water was everywhere. I just had to wait for the drum to fill. Instead I watched Mom.

Living with her had always been like living with a stranger. It's always been the same stranger, one who's lived with me for as long as I can remember. She hardly ever looks directly at me and never says my name. Sometimes she calls Andy "kiddo," like a yard narc would, in a way that means all kids are the same.

I hate her so much that if some idiot fell asleep on me while smoking, the hatred would leak out of me until it poured over the threshold and flooded the streets.

The vac tank was full again and heavy. I started dragging it toward the door when the light went out.

The lamp in Mom's room was one of those old green-glass ones with the long bulb underneath, like they have at the library. It was sitting on a bulging cardboard box in the corner, another one that she had never unpacked. I sighed and turned off the vacuum.

I walked to the bathroom and looked up at the fixture over the mirror. The glass cover was gone, but the two bare bulbs were there. I wasn't sure one of them would fit in the lamp, but it might. I reached up in the dark and unscrewed one.

I took it back into the bedroom and went over to the lamp.

Mom stood where she was. I wished for a second that I could tell her to turn on the vacuum and do some of the work herself, but I didn't say it. I picked up the lamp and looked under the green-glass shade. I hoped it was the bulb and nothing more. I put my hand on the bulb to unscrew it and my hand stuck there.

My jaw locked. My hands curled into fists that couldn't let go. I felt a terrible buzzing all over, down to my bones. I was stuck. I screamed through my teeth and my left hand came bashing down on the lamp without my asking it to.

Andy must have heard me screaming and come back down. He yanked the lamp cord out of the wall, and everything unlocked. He stood there staring at me with big scared eyes.

"Layla, are you okay? Are you okay?"

I was not okay. The shock was still running through me, and I shook all over. I was too dazed to answer for a few seconds, and I saw pure terror on his face while he waited for me to talk. Is this how Frankenstein made a monster?

"I'm fine, Andy. I'm fine." I turned on Mom. "Didn't you see that?"

She looked up. "What?"

"Just now. With the lamp. Didn't you see that?"

"What are you talking about? Are you going to change the bulb or not?" She was mumbling. Going, going, gone.

I picked up the unplugged lamp and threw it at the wall in front of me, hard. The base of it took a chip out of the paint and the drywall underneath. The green-glass shade bounced off and hit Andy in the face.

I don't know what kind of glass doesn't just break, but it didn't. Not against the wall, and not against my baby brother's teeth. I heard it smack against him and then splat on the wet floor. Andy's hands flew to his mouth, and he started to wail. The monster was made.

I took big, jerky steps toward him. My left foot burned and buzzed.

"Let me see. Let me see. Andy, let me look. I need to see how bad it is."

I tried to pull his hands away from it, but he fought me. There was a tiny dot of blood.

I pried his hand away, and a piece of tooth went tumbling to the floor. It was shockingly big, and I thought for a second I had knocked out one of his front teeth. He had just gotten his permanent front teeth in, and I had wrecked his smile forever.

His right front tooth was broken at a jagged diagonal, making it like a tiny fang that came to a point where it met the other one. It would have been better if it had knocked out altogether.

"It huuuuurts," he wailed, high and nasal. "It hurts it hurts it hurts, Layla."

"I know. I know. I'm so sorry. Andy, I'm so sorry."

I walked him to the bathroom and found the sticky pink bottle of baby cold medicine he took when he had the sniffles. I gave him two droppers full, just hoping it'd stop the pain. He quit crying but kept making this high repeating whine noise that I just couldn't stand. I wanted to shake him, but I felt like I deserved to have to hear it forever.

I took him to bed, still wailing, and made him lie down.

"Andy, you have to sleep. Just close your eyes."

He wailed and moaned, one hand at his mouth.

"Damn it, Andy. I'm sorry, but you just have to deal with it, okay? Just try to think of something else."

No answer. No real answer, anyway. No way to feel better about this, probably ever.

He curled up tight like a shrimp, and I put the blankets over him. My hands and feet felt big and stupid. Climbing down the ladder felt like trying to control a huge, clumsy puppet.

I walked back into the bedroom and Mom was still there, sitting on the wet bed, looking at the floor. Checked out.

I walked closer to her. She was slumped forward, totally glazed over. Vacant, like the windows of an empty house.

"Mom can't come to the phone right now. Can I take a message?

"Mom's not home. Nobody's home." No reaction.

"Nobody's ever home, are they, Mom?"

Nothing. I was right in front of her face. She would have been staring at my belly, if she could see anything. I'd seen her in this state, she'd let mosquitoes feed off her eyelids without moving. I could do anything at all.

I reached out my right hand. It felt sore and tingly, the aftermath of the shock still running through me. I could feel it from my right hand down to my left foot, like a vibration that wouldn't stop. I brought my hand down hard and fast, meaning to hit her in the face but striking her ear, off center and without much force.

Nothing.

I reached back and smacked her again, harder this time and more on the jaw. I leaned down and yelled right in her ear. "Wake up! Snap out of it! Come on!"

I stood there, closer to her than I had been in months, smelling her terrible hobo smell, wanting something to happen.

I wanted something from her I wasn't going to get, but that was how it always was. I remember standing there, wanting to yell or cry or hit her again. Even wanting her to hit me back, just anything.

And then something else hit me: checked-out Mom was better than usual Mom. Either way, nothing I said mattered. Nothing I did mattered. She had nothing to offer. But at least when she was checked out she was harmless. No hot cigarette, no sharp nails. No demands on her nameless children. No waking me up with screams.

Harmless. So I hit her again. She didn't move or make a sound. It was like smacking a piece of raw chicken. It didn't matter and it didn't make me feel better. It didn't fix Andy's tooth and it didn't unshock me. So I dropped my hands. I gave up. She didn't fight, but she won anyway.

I wouldn't cry in front of her. That's been my rule since the night we found her in front of the oven. I went out the sliding glass door and did it outside until I could get it under control.

I left the door open so the water would pour out. I could hear it dripping off the balcony down to the parking lot.

Between that and the bathroom sink, I have lived in a swamp ever since.

A week after that unquiet night, she had nailed two big sheets of plywood over that door so that it couldn't be opened again. Andy's tooth still had a sharp edge where it had broken, and he kept running his tongue over it. My aftershock had faded, and Mom had started sleeping on the couch.

His adopt-me face is going to feature that ugly broken tooth. It's going to cost someone money to fix.

He still remembers that I'm the one who gave it to him. I broke my brother's tooth, and I hit my defenseless mother.

I lie alone in my RV and think about that. And I plan how to take myself to the police station.

Sunday Morning

The trick works on another bus driver. Repeatable results. I walk out to the main drag and catch the first bus after dawn, so the creep factor is increased by the fact that it's still a little dark out. The bus is nearly empty. I sit in the back and enjoy the ride.

The police station is in the old part of town, the one with the arches that they light up at Christmas and the small, cute shops that sell very expensive things. I walk across the square holding the letter for Andy in my hand. All I had was notebook paper in my backpack, so I folded an envelope out of that to cover it. It's addressed to him c/o Officer Benson.

There's a tall man standing at the front desk. He's in uniform. I wasn't expecting that—I thought there would be a receptionist like at any other office. Like a pretty woman who smiles a lot and has a headset.

His name tag says Officer Hinajosa. He doesn't smile.

"Hi. I talked to Officer Benson on the phone, and he said I could leave this for him."

He looks down at me over the desk, and I'm sure he can see my pulse pounding hard in my neck. "Benson?"

"Yeah." I clear my throat, fighting panic. "Yeah, it's for a kid he helped place in foster care." I hold it out to him and realize my hand is going to shake. I put it gently on the counter and lace my fingers together. I look up at him and smile. "Can you give that to him, or put it in his box or whatever?"

He smiles back, but only on one side. "We don't have boxes like teachers, little lady. But I can put it in his locker for him."

"Okay. Thank you." I offer him a little wave and walk quickly, but not too quickly.

In the parking lot, I'm looking for the fastest way out of here. I can't wait for the bus across the street from the police department—if Officer Benson comes in or if someone who saw my video spots me, I'm screwed. I can walk a couple of blocks away to another stop, but I'd like to be off these big, busy main streets.

While I'm standing there, looking up and down the street, Jane Chase and her dad spot me on their way to the front entrance of the station.

Jane's dad draws up short. He looks surprised, but not in a good way. More in the way that dog shit on the sidewalk is a surprise.

I break eye contact immediately and start walking away fast, like I didn't see them and don't know them.

Oh, but Jane sees me. Of course.

"I told you! I told you, Dad! She's not dead. There's no way she'd kill herself. She's right there. God!"

She's got her phone up and she's taking a picture or a video, but all she's getting is my bouncing backpack as I run away. I'm transmogrifying before their eyes: solid into vapor.

The last thing I hear before I'm out of earshot is her dad yelling at her to shut up and get back in the car.

I walk all the way back to my RV. I'm too rattled to get on a bus right now. I feel like running, but I don't. I zigzag through neighborhoods, staying off the main streets. I get turned around and caught up in cul-de-sacs and spirals that loop me back to where I began. I'm hungry and thirsty and freaked out and tired.

I turn my phone back on and let it buzz for a long time while it gets a million texts and voicemails. While those come in, I think about what would happen if I put up a crowdfunding campaign. *Support your local homeless teenager.* Like one of those kids in Africa, but more expensive and probably less satisfying. *For only pennies a day, you can keep Layla Bailey in clean socks and burritos.*

Burritos. My stomach contracts to digest the nothing I've fed it. Ugh, I wish I was at school.

I miss getting free food. I wonder what Andy's getting fed wherever he is. I hope he remembers to tell somebody he's allergic to strawberries. He hasn't been to a doctor in years, so it's not like there are records or anything.

Forty-seven voicemails.

Voicemail is the worst. I don't know why it exists.

I delete most of them—they're CPS and cops and people from school. All asking the same thing. I save four. One is a writer from a gossip/news website who wants to meet with me. She promises not to reveal my location to anyone, and also to buy me dinner. That could be good. Two are from another reporter, this one from the *LA Times.* It's basically the same offer, but the guy delivering it sounds like a douche.

The last one is from a social worker.

"Hi, Layla. This is Michelle Jones with Child Protective Services. I just thought you would like to know that your brother, Andrew, has been placed in a long-term foster home and that he's safe. His foster family says that he asks for you constantly. I think it would be really great if you could visit him to help calm him down and get him adjusted to the idea of staying where he is."

There's a long pause, and I'm thinking fast already. It's a pretty smart message. She's offering something I want. She doesn't mention what will happen to me. She doesn't threaten anything or try to intimidate me. She baits the trap like she knows me.

"And I thought you might like to see him, as well. Give me a call and let me know if we can set this up. I'm in the office today until six." She leaves me her number and her email.

If I were a little dumber, that would work like a charm.

If I were a little smarter, I'd figure out how to see Andy and not end up getting caught.

Just smart enough to survive. For now.

Survival is getting tougher, though. There are cops all over the street where my RV sits. I walk slowly past it instead of making the turn, being totally normal.

Time to evaluate my options. On the rich side of town, behind a big, pretty two-story, there's a tree house that hasn't been used in a long time, by the look of it. I slept in it a couple of times last summer when the nights were warm, but this time of year I couldn't make it without a sleeping bag. I know a couple of twenty-four-hour cafés where I can order a tea and sit all day, but I don't even have tea money. For just a second, I remember that Mom thought I had $400.

I wish. I wonder whose money she was looking for then. Did she leave with a bunch of rent money? I always wondered if that would happen after she took the apartment-manager job.

The best choice right now is stuff that's close to home. That's dangerous, but it might be my only shot. I've got the code to Mom's office, if it hasn't been changed. And I've got the master key that opens all the laundry rooms and the room where the pool chemicals are stored. Bonus: Mom's office has a computer I can use.

There's always the library. They're open, and they also have computers and the internet, but they get really snippy if you fall asleep there. Also high risk for being seen.

Sighing, I head toward Mom's office. It has a water cooler and a coffee machine. The fact that there's anything there that I can put in my mouth is the deciding vote. Autotrophs feed themselves. Like me. I wish I could photosynthesize.

I walk the whole complex, but in a crafty way. The door to our old apartment has yellow "Caution" tape across it. The AC unit is gone, and there's a piece of plywood over the hole.

The laundry rooms are all full, since it's the weekend and everybody's catching up on wash while they can. I come around Mom's office on the far side, where there's a tiny window, up really high behind the desk. I climb up on the hose spigot and peer in.

Empty.

Everything is still turned on in there. I signed out of all my accounts, of course, but nobody else is signed in. I don't know if Mom has been back or not, or if they've replaced her. I doubt both of those things.

I drink cup after waxy little cup of water out of the cooler. I set up the coffee machine to make me two cups at once, and I sugar and cream them both until they're white and thick and sweet.

I email the reporter whose questions sounded reasonable.

Hey Erica,

I would like to talk with you today. Here are my conditions:

You have to come alone. Meet me at the Golden Dragon Buffet on Magnolia. Pay for two and give them the name Amber for me. Get a seat near the front windows. I'll be there at 2pm. You can record me yourself, but no other people. I'll answer any questions you have about the video and about myself.

I read in history class that reporters have to protect their sources. That means you can't ambush me with cops or CPS. Just in case you're thinking about it, I can promise you I know this place like the back of my hand and I'll disappear.

I hope we understand each other.

Layla Bailey

I've had three Thanksgivings, two Christmases, and one Easter dinner at the Golden Dragon Buffet. Also a handful of paydays when Mom wanted to take us out, plus the two times Andy and I snuck in, blending in with a bunch of kids on busy days. It's always open, it's cheap, and they don't try to chase you out even though it's been five hours and your little brother is dangerously close to throwing up after eating an entire plate of cream-cheese wontons. I know how to get in and out of that place. Also, I can eat until I bust and survive on that for two more days. Maybe pocket some pork buns for later.

I'm nervous about talking to her. The feeling of being naked on the internet forever is not getting better.

Mom's computer is humming now, waking up and turning on its fan. Over on YouTube, my video has over a million views. There are comments below it in languages I can't read, and trolls and saints and all kinds of people with opinions on my life. I can't stay long there, but my eye keeps going back to the number.

One million people.

On to Twitter.

I have too many notifications to make sense of. I can't reply to everybody, and I know this office won't stay safe for long. I slurp my hot, sweet coffee and get to work.

@airyoddknee: First things first, I'm not dead.

@airyoddknee: Second, I can't answer all of my DMs or reply to all requests. Sorry, too busy and not in a safe place to use the internet.

@airyoddknee: Next up, I don't care about @angel-face787's Instagram. She's bullied me since I moved to this town. I'm used to her shit.

@airyoddknee: I definitely would not kill myself based on what @angelface787 thinks of me. #nevergonnahappen

@airyoddknee: I have no idea where my mother is. I kind of know where CPS put my brother, and at least I know he's safe.

@airyoddknee: Andy, if you're reading this, I love you. I want to see you, and I'm working on that.

@airyoddknee: If Andy's foster parents are reading this: he's allergic to strawberries and gets scared at night. He needs help practicing reading. He loves tacos.

I finish one coffee and start another. My stomach hurts. Folgers and fear. I'm grinding my teeth and watching the door.

@airyoddknee: I don't know what's gonna happen.

@airyoddknee: I hope to get back to #BrookhurstJHS
and resume classes and maintain my grades.
Can somebody tell my teachers I'll be back and
I'm doing the reading?

Replies are already flooding in. I want to just keep tweeting, but
they roll up at the bottom of my screen and I can't ignore them.

@ryguyshyguy: look whos back from the dead
@airyoddknee @angelface787 @macktheknife
@amberdextrous

@jen_valenti: @airyoddknee pls come to the school,
we can put you in touch with people who can
help. #BrookhurstJHS #FindLayla

@angelface787: I fucking TOLD YOU GUYS RT@airyod-
dknee: First things first, I'm not dead.

@AnaheimPD: @airyoddknee please contact us, we can
help you. #FindLayla

@dolanarmy: i can find ur mom i promise @airyoddknee

@blue_id_3: .@airyoddknee what an attention whore.
#FindLayla #tcot #yolo #sorrynotsorry

@iguanabarf: @airyoddknee were u kidnapped tho?

@Kristi_the_poet: @airyoddknee I will totes pass on ur
msg to teachers <3 p.s. you can come here #bff

Almost finished.

> @airyoddknee: You'll be hearing from me soon. Watch
> for a news story. #FindLayla

It is so weird to hashtag my own name. I finish my coffee, despite my stomachache. One last check of my email. Erica must watch hers constantly.

> Hey Layla,
>
> 2pm sounds great. I'm leaving LA now. See you
> then.

She leaves me her phone number at the bottom.

I throw away my cups, sign out, and shut down. I hate the glass in here. I wish I had a place with no windows. Maybe underground. One door with one key, no leaks. No dread of Mom cycling in and out of herself in ways I can't predict or anticipate. Someplace to feel safe.

Does that feeling even exist? No, it exists. I've seen the calm of other biomes. I've stolen it, like a parasite. What I don't know is whether I can get my own and maintain it. Peace and homeostasis look expensive.

I walk behind the strip mall, where I won't be in view of passing cars. There are small places where I can be invisible. The backsides of buildings are for dumpster divers and deliveries, but most of the time there's nobody back there.

In fact, there's nobody out back except the cook from the Mexican place two doors down, outside having a smoke. He smokes menthols like Mom, and I have to get past him fast, because the smell makes me want to throw up my coffee. I sit against the stucco behind the buffet part of the building and read about Mendel and his peas. I think about what I've inherited and what's just mine. I look at the Punnett squares and think about how Andy doesn't look like me. I think about his broken tooth, and then I want to stop reading. But I've got to stay focused on something. I have a few hours to burn.

1:45 p.m.

I head around to the front entrance, the plastic gold pagoda roof over the glass double doors. The winter sunlight is no joke today. It's cold but bright, so most of the shades are down at the front tables. I walk past once and don't see anyone who I think might be Erica. I walk all the way to the end of the strip mall and stand at the corner of it until I've counted to a hundred. I turn around and walk to the other end. I stand there, singing the little song that names the first fifty elements of the periodic table. My hands are sweaty. I rub them on my jeans and then regret it, thinking to wipe them on my back pockets next time. But that's not really different, it's just that I can't see it.

With my back to the door, I'm going over what I can say to the reporter when she asks me.

My brother, Andy, is the most important—no, *he's the only thing. Andy is vitally*—no.

I never intended to cause this much . . . I first set out to just tell my story. I never thought I would . . .

Andy and I grew up in a terrible place with our mother, who was . . . what? How do I explain Mom to anyone? They'd never believe anybody was really like that. *She had a job and could lie convincingly to anyone who asked too many questions.*

She won't ask me about Mom. She'll ask me about the video.

I made that video to tell the truth . . . to tell the truth in a way that nobody could fail to understand. Evidence can't lie. I made that video so that someone would have to believe me.

I'm muttering to myself. Like Mom. I stop. I walk again.

I'm walking back again when I see a woman beeping the alarm on a cute little green car. She carelessly flings shiny black hair out of her face and pushes her sunglasses up the bridge of her nose.

No kids and no old people with her. If she goes into the Dragon, it's her.

It's her.

I wait a few seconds and call her phone. Walking past the window, I turn my head to look in. She's pulling her phone out of her purse to look at it. I hang up.

Once she's paid and sitting down, I walk in carrying my backpack in one hand.

"Hi, my aunt already paid for me? It should be under Amber?"

"Oh yeah, she's sitting by the beverage bar." The hostess points, and I follow her finger.

Erica is already watching.

I walk over to her and it seems to take forever. I feel little muscle jumps in my abdomen. I hold my hand out as I approach.

"Hi, Erica? I'm Layla."

She shakes my hand for a minute, looking closely at my face. "Yes, you are. I was worried you were another fake. It's great to meet you. Won't you sit down?"

The smell of the hot chafing dishes is making me want to ignore her and hunt like the animal I am. "Actually, I'm gonna grab some food real quick."

"Oh, of course." She looks back at her phone as she slides into the red vinyl booth. I shoulder my backpack again and load up a plate. I carry it and a cup of cold tea back to her.

"Okay, sorry about that. Just really hungry."

"Of course, no problem." She's not eating anything, even though she paid to get in.

Between bites I tell her, "It's okay, you can still ask me stuff."

"Okay." She lays her smartphone down on the table between us, and the screen shows an old-fashioned microphone with a red dot. "Layla Bailey, may I have your permission to record our interview so that I can assure accuracy when I quote you?"

"Sure." My cheek is filled with fried rice.

"One more time, more clearly." She seems a little bit amused. I don't know why I like her, but I do. We smile a little at each other when I swallow.

"Sorry. Yeah, you have my permission to record us talking. Yes."

"Great. And you are?"

"Layla Louise Bailey."

"The girl from the biome video."

"Yeah, that's me," I tell her, feeling silly.

"How did you come up with the idea for that video?" She's looking right at me. I feel weird eating while she watches. I finish chewing and set my fork down for a minute.

"I . . . I just thought about how each organism interacts with its environment, like we were studying in biology. And I realized that my environment was different from most people's, and that it was kind of interesting."

She blinks her big brown eyes slowly, like a cat. "So you knew your house was unusual."

"Well, yeah. I mean, I've got friends. And TV and the internet. I know that's not how most people live."

"Are you embarrassed at all, now that it's out there and so many people have seen it?"

My face goes hot like I shoved it under the sneeze guard over the steaming dishes of sweet-and-sour pork. Being seen by all those people online is different from someone saying it to my burning face.

"I am, yeah. It's weird. It's like being . . . exposed. Like everyone knows something about me that used to be secret. Like when nudes leak, I guess. But it's the truth, and I needed to tell it. So I told."

Erica relaxes a little bit, sitting back in her booth and looking at her phone. "Where is the rest of your family? Isn't there anybody out there who you would like to reach out to?"

"I think I have some cousins in Missouri? I don't know. I know my grandparents died a long time ago. We've never really had much contact with any relatives." I hardly ever think about that. I can't imagine my mom having a mom.

"And your father?"

"I barely remember him. I know he was in the Army."

"Interesting. And you're how old?" She's looking me over like she's trying to guess.

I wipe my face. "How old do I look?"

She smiles a little. I think she's about thirty. "I wouldn't sell you beer. You have a way about you that makes you seem older. I think that's just your life, honestly. I have to tell you, I know from the police information on you that you're fourteen."

"I'll be fifteen on the winter solstice."

"That's a cool birthday."

"Yeah. When's yours?"

"Oh, in the summer. June seventeenth. I always have my party at the beach."

"Cool."

She's writing something down on a tablet with her stylus, but I can't see the screen. "Yeah, I think so. So what do you want to be when you grow up?"

"A scientist. I'd really like to work in a lab that studies weird living things. Slime molds. Or viruses."

"You're gonna be in college for a long time." She's smiling at me over her tablet. I smile back.

"Yeah, I know. That's alright, though."

I'm watching her very closely. All previous experiments in trust have failed. That doesn't mean that they always will, but statistically I feel like my hypothesis here is solid.

126

I'm thinking about the types of relationships we learned about in biology: parasitic versus symbiotic. This could work like symbiosis, both of us getting something we need out of this conversation. She looks harmless. Like she's just trying to get to know me. I'm less nervous than I was in the beginning. Talking to a reporter isn't as bad as I thought it would be. I eat an egg roll fast while the filling is still hot and take a drink to wash it down. I'm thinking about a second plate when I realize she's watching me again.

I look up. The look in her eyes is focused, like she's not eating because she's planning on eating *me*.

She's been working on me to make me less nervous. I get it now. Not like Jane works on me, and not like teachers sometimes do. It's a totally new feeling, and I don't know what to call it. Parasitic, I realize. Not symbiotic. Mimicry—a venomous animal pretends to be a harmless one to get you close enough to bite. Camouflaged until I looked at her eyes instead of her eyespots for the first time.

What are my defenses?

Erica is keen, eyes focused forward. "So, when you made the video, what was in your mind? What were you hoping to get out of it?"

The waitresses don't bring anything to the table at the Dragon except tea, which arrives in no-handle green mugs that look like fat bamboo. I pour two sugar packets into mine and swirl the hot tea, staring down into it. I watch the sugar dissolve slowly, in a white grainy sweep at the bottom.

"I was hoping to find a new home. I know how stupid that sounds, like something a Disney orphan says just before the brave animal friend leads them to their new parents or whatever. But there are those commercials on TV with the sad music and the skinny dogs and sick cats in their dirty cages, and people call in with their credit-card numbers or show up to the shelter to adopt some three-legged puppy. So I kind of thought I could show my own living conditions and the same kind of thing could happen."

Meg Elison

Erica doesn't say anything, but it looks hard for her. She's waiting. I can feel my throat closing up, so I take a sip of tea.

"I wanted something I can't really have, which is a safe, clean place where I can take care of my brother while I finish high school. I know CPS will probably find him a home."

"And you? Why not let them find you a home? They can try and put you guys together, you know."

"I guess."

"You guess what?"

There's still sugar left at the bottom of my tea. I can't look up. I shouldn't tell her this. This is not symbiosis. But I can't stop. I want to tell the truth of it.

"Nobody is going to want me. Andy's little, and he can still be somebody's kid. I made that video with my report card to show people that I'm not a fuckup. I'd be fine if somebody could offer me a closet to sleep in, and I won't burn down their house or go to jail or anything, but I can't become part of somebody's family. Andy is gonna be like one of those baby monkeys that gets released into the wild and the other monkeys accept him and he forgets there was ever a before-time. I won't ever forget, because it's been my whole life. I'll always be weird, like one of those gorillas that learned too much sign language to go back to the forest."

I drink and drink and look down. I can't say anything for a minute. I wanted to sound like a scientist. I wanted to describe my observations without having feelings about them. But I'm the subject and the observer, and there's no way to separate me from me. The blue-ringed octopus is back, and I can't fight it.

"You know, lots of people don't think you're a fuckup."

I don't say anything.

Her tone of voice is totally different. Before, it was like she could get something out of me if she squeezed just right, if she poked the right spot. Now it's softer, like when the school nurse first met me and didn't know I was gonna be a regular. Not symbiosis. Sympathy.

"In fact, your social worker told me that she has a list of people who saw your video who really want you to come live with them."

I drink my tea until that last sip that's almost all sugar.

"They don't know what they're signing up for."

"Foster parents have seen a lot, actually. Lots worse than you, I'm sure. Kids with arrest records and brain damage and . . ." She trails off and looks out the window.

I stare into my empty cup.

She taps the red button on her phone and stops the recording.

"Okay, Layla. Listen to me. Are you listening?"

I can't look at her. "Yes."

"Look, I went through some bad shit when I was younger. I was out on my own when I was not much older than you, because my mom found out about my girlfriend. You follow?"

"Yeah, I follow." I wonder if I can drink her tea.

She's staring me down like she needs me to hear this way more than she needs to say it.

"It seems like the worst thing that has ever happened, and that nothing will ever get any better, and that you'll always be what you are right now. That's all bullshit. It gets better."

More than sympathy. Empathy, I guess. "Oh my god, you're doing that YouTube meme thing about gay kids." I'm drinking her tea. She doesn't stop me.

"Yeah, I am." She fiddles with her tablet again. "But it's not just about being gay. It's about getting bullied or being poor or being just really weird. The point is, this is probably the worst it's ever going to be. You're going to make it through this. You're going to get a better shot than other kids who aren't as smart as you, whose videos didn't go viral. You're having a moment. That's why I'm talking to you today."

She hits the button on her phone again. We're recording.

"So. So if people who are interested in fostering you or even adopting you read my article today, what do you want them to know about you?"

I swallow hard. I watch two girls in matching outfits elbow each other at the ice-cream machine, fighting for who gets to go first. My phone buzzes in my pocket and I pull it out. My Twitter is blowing up again. I forgot that I had signed my phone into the Dragon's Wi-Fi once before. It must have connected automatically. The first notification stops my breathing, and I'm feeling the effect of Erica's venom already.

> @angelface787: You guys, you know Layla made this whole thing up, right? #FindLayla

> @angelface787: She's just trying to get attention. She filmed that whole video in an old abandoned house, I can show it to you. @CNN @MSNBC @Gawker #FindLayla

> @angelface787: she's just a weird emo tryna get famous

> @angelface787: ya I said it @airyoddknee

> @Kristi_the_poet: wtf Jane?

> @angelface787: .@Kristi_the_poet ur always defending her because you're in on it #FindLayla

> @angelface787: .@airyoddknee everyone is going to know how fake you are

> @angelface787: hey @ericamalkasian when you talk to her, remember what I told you

I tap on Erica's handle and look back over her timeline for a minute. "Layla?"

Ignoring her, I roll backward through her replies from the last few days. She's been talking to a bunch of people who say they're me. Most of them are using stills from my video for avis, but a couple of them have my school picture from fifth grade.

> @ericamalkasian: @angelface787 can you show me that abandoned house?
>
> @angelface787: @ericamalkasian totes dm me your number
>
> @ericamalkasian: @angelface787 done

Erica has been talking to Jane. To Kristi. To people at my school that I don't even know, who say they know me. She doesn't believe me. I'm cold all over, cold like that night in the bathtub never ended. I open my mouth and nothing comes out.

Of all the people in the world who could tell her something about me, she had to talk to Jane Chase. Jane Chase who pinched my nipple one day and pointed out to everyone that I didn't have anything on under my sweater. We were nine. Jane who would comment loudly on how fast I ate my lunch, or announce that she had seen my shoes on the shelf at the dollar store. Jane who lied to teachers, telling them I stole her Valentine's Day cards so that I had to give her all of mine. Jane the predator. Erica the parasite.

And Erica doesn't mention any of this to me at all. I should have known.

She's looking at me expectantly. "What's the matter?" Annoyed.

I don't say anything. I don't have many natural defenses, but that one never fails.

Erica turns her chin a little to one side like she's recovering from a bad taste in her mouth. She looks over her notes. "In your video you said, 'I'll do chores. I'll be quiet. If you've got a garage or a laundry room I could sleep in, I am mostly housebroken.' Is all of that still true?"

"Everything I said was true. Everything." A little too forceful.

"Layla, it's okay. Just tell my readers what you want most."

"I want to get out of here."

"What?" She looks up at me again.

"You think I made this up. What did Jane tell you? No, wait. It doesn't even matter. I don't care." I am picking up my bag and sliding out of the booth.

"What? Layla, wait. Come back here."

Maybe it's my imagination, but I could swear heads turn our way when she says my name.

"Just make up whatever you want. Or ask Jane about my life. Why did you even . . . I have to go."

"Layla, wait! Who texted you?"

She's gathering her things, trying to catch up to me. I wish she'd stop saying my name.

I slip through the line at the front door and bolt for the street. Traffic opens up just right, and I'm across the street and into the court-yard of an office building before I can catch my breath. I sit down behind a huge air conditioner that's humming so loud I can't hear myself breathing. Why's it running in December? I think hard about that before I open my phone again.

@angelface787: if #FindLayla was telling the truth, she'd answer me

Alright. Fine.

@airyoddknee: @angelface787 is Jane Alice Chase,
that's the truth

@airyoddknee: she's the worst bully I've ever had, and
I've been to a lot of schools

@airyoddknee: and anybody who thinks @angel-
face787 is right can watch my next video

@airyoddknee: I'm not getting anything out of this. I'm
cold and tired, and I don't have a coat or a safe
place to sleep. Why would I make this up?

@angelface787: cuz ur as crazy as your mom
@airyoddknee

@ericamalkasian: @airyoddknee please call me. I'd like
to finish our interview.

If I break this phone, I'll never get another one. I have to put it
down to make sure I don't throw it against a wall.

I don't know I'm crying until I feel it rolling off my chin and into
my shirt. I wasn't allowed to cry in front of Mom since I was a baby, so
it always feels like a hot octopus is ripping my feelings out of my throat.
The octopus strangles me and the AC unit kicks off. It's quiet except
for the sound of cars on the road. Getting the octopus off me is hard. I
think about its name, its poison, its habitat. If I know it, I can control
it. I think about all the Chinese food Erica just bought me. Nobody
can take that away, at least.

I open my phone again to tell Jane I'll show her. She's beat me
to it.

> @angelface787: alright @airyoddknee, meet me and
> we'll see who's faking. I'll DM the place and
> time.

A bunch more tweets from Erica and I'm really glad that I didn't give her my phone number. I can't see my DMs or notifications once I get away from the Dragon's Wi-Fi signal. I'm going to have to find a computer to figure this out.

I lie my way onto another bus to head to the last library I know I haven't visited lately. The whole way there, I'm trying to figure out what I'm going to do. What I want to do is set Jane on fire and post a video of me pointing and laughing, but that won't prove anything other than that bitches be cold but also flammable.

5:45 p.m.

By the time we reach the library, I have three pages of DMs, and I have to dig to find one from Jane.

> @angelface787 has sent you a direct message!

> Meet me in the parking lot of the old Walmart in the
> bad part of town, tomorrow at sundown. I can
> prove you're a fake.

I message her back and tell her I'll be there. I plug my phone and camera in, sitting on the floor in a corner of the library behind the reference books that haven't been touched since before I was born. I read two whole books before they start flipping the light switches to tell us that we don't have to go home, but we can't stay here.

It's dark out, and I have no plan for where I'm going to sleep tonight. I unplug and pack up slowly, enjoying my last few moments of light and heat. I feel like I haven't slept in a year.

I walk for what seems like hours, wishing I had been able to check a book out. I've read everything in my backpack twice.

The minute I spot the *lavandería*, I know what it is. I've been in a thousand of them in my life, bored to tears, pushing Andy around in one of those death-trap carts and waiting for our clothes to get done. Our last apartment and the Valencia Inn didn't have their own laundry rooms, so we used to come to these when all our clothes had been worn twice and our socks were gray. Every single one is the same: The machines are huge and old and loud. The tile floor is sticky. The fluorescent lights buzz overhead and never go out, and there will be at least one loud TV chained to a corner of the ceiling.

The signs are in Spanish, but I know "Open 24 Hours" when I see it in any language. I also know that there are moms in there at all hours, and that people will assume I belong to one of them if I doze off on a bench.

Sure enough, there are two women at opposite ends of the bright, humming room. They both look as tired as I feel, and one of them has a baby in a carrier that she checks out nervously every few minutes. I turn my backpack around to my front and sit down on the bench nearest the TV, which is on mute and I am so thankful.

When I wake up, I don't know what time it is, but I do know I'm in trouble. The women are gone. The humming has stopped. And there's a man on the bench next to me.

I don't move. He doesn't know I'm awake yet, and if I don't move maybe nothing will happen.

He moves a little closer to me. Looks toward the glass front of the building. Scoots closer again.

My hearing is so sharp. I hear his ragged breathing, the shaggy inhale and exhale like someone on a bike chugging hard uphill, hoping to coast on the way down. I can see every speck of dirt and crumb on the floor. I can see the hairs sprouting out of the back of his hand, single and double and crawling up toward his wrist.

I sit up straight and wrap my arms around my backpack in front of me.

"Hi." He says it oddly, like we know each other.

"Hi." I won't look at him.

His voice stays low and familiar. "You're here all alone."

"My dad must have gone out to the car. I'm sure he'll be right back."

I can feel him looking out the window again. He looks a long time.

This isn't the first time a grown-up man has noticed that I'm alone and he could probably get whatever he wanted from me without much trouble. I tense up all over. I'm as hard and sharp as the stinger on a *Clistopyga crassicaudata*. I'm ready.

"There's no cars in the lot. Nobody's out there."

"I better go, then." I stand up quick, all in one motion, taking as big a step as I can away from this guy and still not looking at him. I can see his shoes. If there's no cars in the lot, where did he come from? If he puts a hand on me, I plan to twist away and scream.

"Go where?"

"Go home." I start toward the door, keeping the pack in front of me. I know he's standing up, he's coming after me. I don't know this neighborhood. I don't know where I'll run or hide, and it's got to be too late for the bus. I have to get out of here, it doesn't matter where.

A few more sticky squares of tile to the door. I'm not running, but I will be soon. I can see him in the lit reflection of the glass front wall. He's close.

"Hey," he says, and I can see he's reaching toward me and it's like a nightmare and I can't look back or I'll get trapped here. "Hey, do you need a ride home? Or how about some money? I could give you some money."

I hate the sweetness of his voice. It would be better if he was scary, I could run and be sure that anyone would agree with me that he was a bad guy. He's trying to seem like a nice guy so that I'll turn around, I'll say yes and go along. All those times in school when they said that strangers would offer us candy or puppies. They should have told us these guys are a lot smarter than that.

He's right behind me. I can feel him breathing. This is it.

"No, I don't need any money. I have to go. Bye."

I'm running out the door, vision adjusting slowly from the bleach-white lights inside to the dingy yellow lights outside. There's no traffic at all. It's so quiet I can hear him holding the creaky glass door open, not following me, calling after me, making another offer.

I don't look back.

Monday Dawn

I think I got a few hours of sleep in the *lavandería*, but I am obviously never sleeping again. I walked after that until I was back in familiar territory. I sit in the bathroom of a Denny's for a while, trying to get myself together.

I think back to when I had a bedroom. To my biome. I feel like I'm being watched everywhere now.

To get breakfast, I pull one of my dumbest and riskiest tricks. I wait for a family with a couple of kids to finally give up on their children ever eating and pack them up to leave. The dad takes them out to the car, and the mom pays the check at the register. As soon as she's out the door, I'm at their table.

This only works if nobody sees me sit down. The one waitress in the room has her back turned to me, filling coffees. I have a few minutes.

Parents always tell their kids to finish their food because there are starving people in Africa or Southeast Asia or somewhere, but I'm glad that most of the kids don't listen, because I'm starving right here. I learned to pull this trick when I was really little, before Andy was even born. Mom would buy a cup of coffee and read a newspaper for hours. I would slip away to other tables, as sneaky and quick as a little rat. Sometimes it works where adults have been, but I've tested it fewer times. I look like I belong at a messy table where kids have sat. And the best bet is always other kids. They leave behind big messes of pancake syrup and scrambled eggs with cheese and ketchup. Even the best eaters miss whole slices of toast. Mom would pick up tips, quick as a magician, and make them disappear. We were a pair of thieves back then.

Today's table is pretty good. A little ham-and-egg sandwich left, a couple of big swallows of orange juice and coffee. The littlest kid smeared oatmeal all over the table, that's no good to me. The mom left her whole fruit cup—think of the starving children, Mom. I'm already standing as I get the last slice of somebody's whole-wheat toast wrapped in a napkin and stuffed in my pocket. The waitress is gone back to the kitchen, and my eyes slide over her tip money: six dollars folded neatly under a coffee cup.

"I could give you some money."

I leave it and walk quickly out the door. I'm only stealing food that would have gone into the trash. If I take that money, if I say yes to some guy who offers me money, I become somebody else. Somebody like Mom.

Not today.

The whole day lies ahead of me, and all I want to do is sleep. I have nowhere to be until sundown. Now that I've eaten, my eyes feel heavy, and I know I'm gonna fall asleep soon whether I want to or not.

Too sleepy to think. *Think.* Where can I sleep safely and be left alone?

The RV hasn't seemed like a good idea since all those cops were there. I miss that little loft with a pain in my chest like it was my home since birth. The tree house is a bad option in broad daylight. The library won't let me sleep there, and the ones I know best might spot me and know who I am. Mom's office can't possibly be safe anymore, and if my laundry-room keys still work, daytime is not a good bet for them, either.

But the laundry keys open one other thing.

I think Andy and I spent more time in the pool than in our house. The water is cloudy today. It doesn't look like the filter is working or anybody has added chlorine in a while. Mom sent me to do it more than once when the maintenance man couldn't make it.

Really, it was a pool that got me interested in science. Not this pool, but our first one when we moved to California. Mom got a job as a custodian at a fancier apartment complex, and she had to take care of the pool. She took us with her some days, I don't know why. The times when she was nice to us made even less sense than when she'd just check out or leave us home alone. Andy would swim around and around in the little baby pool while Mom showed me how to skim the water with a net, how to clean the leaves out of the filter trap. We found live ducks and frogs in the pool sometimes. The ducks I could just scare away, but the frogs I'd have to catch. There was one swimming in circles, one day. *Pseudacris cadaverina*, maybe. It was pale, not green like I expected.

"Mom?"

"Yeah?" She was arching away from the long handle of the pool skimmer, trying to get something from the middle of the surface.

"Why doesn't the chlorine kill the frog?" I was trying to catch it in my bare hands. It was slippery and quick.

"It only kills little things. Bacteria. Not big things, like frogs or people." Her cigarette hung from the corner of her mouth, and her forehead was scrunched up. She saw that I had caught the frog and released it gently into a planter with a sago palm, *Cycas revoluta*, in it. "Go get the test."

The test was a little plastic square with a vial stuck to either side. It came in a bigger plastic box that held the little yellow and red droppers. I brought it to her expectantly. I couldn't wait to see how it worked.

Mom filled the vials with pool water and then added drops slowly. The water on the left turned pale yellow.

"See that? The pool needs chlorine." She tapped a long, jagged fingernail on the miniature color chart that showed the acceptable color range and pH numbers. I nodded. I saw.

She dropped a little red into the vial on the right. "And it needs acid. See the pH level is almost eight?" She held up the test, and the sunlight caught it. For a second, I was living some other life where my mom was a scientist and showing me the laboratory.

After she'd showed me, I always ran the test. It felt important. I was keeping the pool safe.

I would never jump into this cloudy pool I'm looking at today. I step on the broken fence to open the gate and look around. It's too early, nobody is swimming. No frogs, no ducks. Casually, I try my key in the utility-room door.

It still works.

I feel like I ought to do something to earn my space. In the utility closet, I pull a big scoop of chlorine from the bucket. I walk back into the sunlight and throw the granules out into the deep end, my arm making a wide arc just like Mom's. I go back and get another scoop of diatomaceous earth and dump it in the filter, just like she taught me. Mostly when the water is cloudy, that's what it needs. I don't have to test it to know that.

When that's done, I lock myself into the utility room. Really, it's a closet and I have to shove pool chemicals and buckets around to get enough room to lie down. There's a pile of old red awnings in there, though, from some attempt years ago to pretty this place up. That must have been about as convincing as tying a bow around a toilet, but I'm glad they're in here. I lie on top of most of them and under the last one. They're dirty, and something I can't really see crawls away when I shake the top one, and I don't care at all. I am no stranger to *Blattella germanica*.

I get the best sleep I've ever had.

When I wake up, I turn my phone on to see what time it is. Wi-Fi from some nearby unprotected router gives me a weak signal. I've slept all day, and people on Twitter are predicting that I won't show up.

But I don't have anywhere else to be.

Sundown

The sky is deep orange with flat purple clouds by the time I walk to the old Walmart. I eat my slice of pocket toast on the way there, wondering if I can go back to the pool room tonight. I've never stayed in a nice hotel, but I bet that's what it's like. Perfect. Dark. Warm. Secure.

Well, nice hotels obviously have lights that work, and you don't have to sleep with buckets of chlorine and acid all around you. But you get the idea.

There's a small crowd in the parking lot. So this must be the right place. I'm already filming. The walk up will be bumpy, and I'm going to have to give it to Kristi to edit.

Hopefully she'll do it for me.

She's the first one I see. She's chewing her lip nervously, and she's holding hands with Emerson Berkeley, with his shy smile and their coordinated black hoodies.

Fuck them both.

Amber Rodin tosses her curly hair to one side in the wind, as if to call attention to how great it is.

Mackenzie Biros is holding a camera just like mine, standing right next to Jane. Jane is obviously prepared to appear on camera. Her makeup looks like something an Instagram influencer would do. I put my camera down and realize my hands are filthy. There's black under my fingernails, and my face . . .

I hold the camera up and get a shot of my own face, turning the viewer around so that I can see it.

I look like I literally rolled in dirt. #selfie. Checking myself out would have been a great idea a few hours ago. Now there's nothing I can do.

Paul DeMarco has to be the one to say it, though. Because of course he does.

"You look like you slept in a dumpster."

Jane rolls her eyes. "She did that on purpose. She's trying to look pathetic so that we believe her story."

Ryan Audubon is staring at me, but not in the way that he usually stares at me. It's like he has a soul in there somewhere.

"What?" I bark it at him.

"You . . . you look really skinny."

Mackenzie pans the camera toward him.

"I mean, you're always skinny. But right now, like your *face* is skinny."

Jane to the rescue, once again. "So? She could be on a diet to make herself look skinny and sad. Okay, let's start."

She clears her throat, and Mackenzie turns the lens toward her face.

"I'm Jane Chase, and I've known Layla Bailey for like four years now. She has always been a drama queen, telling stories about me to try and get me in trouble. Her recent viral video went way beyond what she usually does, trying to make it look like her mom is some kind of monster and she was like a prisoner in this rotting house. Layla, how did you do it? How did you fake that whole video?"

Mackenzie turns the camera to me, and for a minute I'm sure this video is going to go viral too because I'm going to beat everyone in this parking lot to death. Most of the great apes do that. Chimps have wars. Gorillas tear each other apart. *H. sapiens* is the best at it, but I've never done it before. I'm sure that I can.

Fuck Ryan's pity. Fuck Kristi and Emerson and their hands and their hoodies. Fuck Paul for being here, and fuck Jane for always being Jane. But fuck Mackenzie most of all, for falling in line with whatever

Jane says. Nobody would listen to Jane if she didn't always have these followers around her.

I clear my throat.

"Okay, Jane. You got me. I faked the whole thing."

"That's right! I knew it!" She's holding up her phone, rolling some video she shot. I can see the graffiti of ten-foot-tall dicks on the walls inside those abandoned houses near the freeway. It's not even close to my biome.

"That's pathetic, Jane. That doesn't look anything like my video. Let me tell you how I did it. I'm much better at this than you are."

Mackenzie swings away from Jane and back to me.

"I broke the pipes in my mom's house months ago, to get the leak going. I planted those mushrooms and tended them by hand until they looked perfect, growing out of my brother's dresser. I broke the front door with my massive incredible strength and then I forced my mom to never fix it. I wrecked my own clothes so that I would always look like shit and then I called the power company and told them to turn off our lights."

"In these houses I saw—"

I cut her off so fast that Mackenzie doesn't even have time to turn around. "That's right, Jane. When you met me in fifth grade, I was already tangling up my own hair. I did it on purpose so that you'd call me Brillohead and make me cry. Remember when you did that?"

"That wasn't—" Nope. She's starting to look like this isn't going the way she planned.

"I called the school and demanded free lunches. I gave myself lice over and over just to get some time off. I purposely got my period and bled through my pants that one time so that you could point it out to everyone before I could fix it, and so that everyone would laugh when I got up to leave the room. Remember that, Mackenzie? You were there. In fact, you were all there. That was in last year's gifted class."

144

The boys are looking at the ground as if their eyes have weights in them. Kristi looks ready to cry, but she's so emotional.

"Layla, we didn't all laugh."

"It's okay, Kristi. It doesn't matter. Because I faked the whole thing. Mackenzie, focus on Kristi's face, she looks really dramatic right now."

Kristi buries her head in Emerson's shoulder.

Jane is staring me down behind Mackenzie. If looks could kill, we'd have both died a long time ago. But looks don't kill and words don't hurt and this is all fake, so nothing matters.

"I stayed at school anytime there was a field trip that required money, because it seemed way more fun than the zoo. Remember that time Jane told everyone to put pennies in my desk, Mackenzie? That was hilarious, and I totally faked that. I totally faked being hungry and dirty and unlucky, specifically because it has been so awesome to be the subject of your jokes these last few years. I finally had to stop faking it so hard, because I got sick of laughing so much every day."

Mackenzie lowers the camera and she's crying. "Wait, Layla. You don't—"

"Oh no, Mackenzie. Keep rolling. We're not done here."

"Yes we are. We're done." Jane tries to pull the camera out of her hand, and Mackenzie pushes her off. Kristi and Emerson step toward her, and we're about to fight in this parking lot, all of us. It should have been a fight a long time ago, but I'm glad it's happening today. I'm ready for a fight.

"Jane, I faked my whole life. I faked that day my mom came to the school just so you'd write super funny tweets about it, and I've been faking being on the run since then. But the best thing I made up was you."

She's got her mouth open to talk, but I'm not giving her a second to speak. Ever again.

"I faked having this stupid bitch bully me every day about stuff that wasn't funny or okay to joke about. This was all a really fun game, but I'm done faking it now. You don't exist anymore, and neither do I.

You're going to try to show this video to someone and all that will be there will be ten minutes of silence in this parking lot. I was never here, and neither were you. It was all pretend. You got that, Mackenzie? All clear there? Glad you were a part of it?"

Amber Rodin is crying now, too. "Layla, I'm so sorry. This is so messed up."

"You don't exist, Amber. Neither does your hair." She touches it like she's never noticed it before.

I turn to leave them. I am definitely going back to that pool closet. I want to be buried there.

I hear Jane and Mackenzie struggling over the camera, and I turn to look.

"It's too late. I was streaming it." Mackenzie looks like someone slapped her in the face with a bag of frozen fish sticks.

"Why? What the hell, Mack?" Jane is wresting the camera away from her, and just as Ryan steps in to break them up, red and blue lights churn into the night.

It's perfect. At the exact same time, they all look up at me with the eyes of cartoon characters who see the steamroller pressing toward them. The lights are coming from behind me.

I turn around and face what seems like an army of cops.

Monday Evening

Officially, I was arrested for stealing the camera from the school.

I can't deny it. It was in my hands when the cops took my backpack and searched my pockets. I lost the neoprene case somewhere. They didn't find anything else, though, despite the female officer's repeated questions about whether or not I had drugs.

"If I had drugs, wouldn't I have money?"

"Just answer the question." The cop's voice was more tired than angry.

They brought me to the police station after everyone else's parents came and got them. It was spectacular seeing Bette and Mr. Chase from the back seat of a police car. What I'll never forget is that none of them looked surprised.

The cops didn't book me, and the female officer told me the school probably wouldn't press charges.

Another woman walks in, and I know instantly that she is a social worker. She gets me a glass of water and asks the cops to cut my zip tie off. We sit at a metal table.

"Thanks for getting them to uncuff me." I rub my wrists and take a drink.

"My name is Michelle Jones."

"Layla Bailey. Nice to meet you, Ms. Jones."

She looks at me the way teachers do on the first day. "It's actually Dr. Jones. I usually tell little ones to call me Miss Michelle, but you're not a little one, are you?"

"No."

She keeps looking at me, waiting.

"Should I call you Doc?"

"That'd be fine. I'd like to call you Layla, if that's alright." Her lipstick is just a little bit purple, and I can see that she's trying not to smile.

"That's fine, Doc."

"Alright, first things first. You're not being charged, but you are not free to go."

"How does that work?"

She sets down her tablet and sighs. "I know you've been on your own for a while, and taking care of yourself for a while before that. But the fact is, you're a minor. So until we figure out if you have any family, you're going to have to go into foster care."

"Oh." My water glass is empty.

"Now, I know you don't like the sound of that. I watched your video, and I can tell you that every single foster family house in the system will be nicer than where you were living. I know some nice people who can provide you with your own room. They'll take you today."

"I want to see my brother, Andy. Can you arrange that?"

She nods, looking at her tablet. "Yes, I thought that might be a priority for you. So, listen. I can arrange for you to see him as early as tomorrow, but I need something from you."

I look up at her eyes. As brown as mine, as my mother's, but so different.

"What?"

"You're a smart kid. You have the skills to be a successful runaway. It's really easy for you to disappear, right?"

No use lying to her. "Right."

"I need you to give me your word that you won't do that to these people. I'm going to take you to my favorite foster family—I mean these are the nicest people I've ever met. They are really good to the kids I bring there. But I'm gonna do that, and I'm gonna bring your little brother over for dinner, if and only if you promise me not to slip out in the middle of the night and scare them. Will you stay put?"

What happens to bad foster kids? You're already in the place where you go when nobody wants you. Where do you go after that?

I want to tell her that I'll do whatever I need to do. That I won't promise anything, and be a total badass runaway. But I'm so tired of everything and everyone. I want something different. I don't know what it is, but my current methods aren't producing the desired result. I have to do something different to get something different. So I nod.

"Doc, I'm really hungry. And tired. And it's probably pretty obvious how bad I need a shower. I will totally stay put with people who will help me out with any of that."

"I need your word, Layla." She's got me pinned down with her brown eyes.

"Do you want me to sign something?"

She laughs a little. "You can't sign anything, honey. You're a minor. I want you to tell me you promise and shake my hand."

I hold out my hand. "I promise I will not run away from a nice foster home where there is a shower and some food, and you promise you will bring me my brother."

She takes my dirty hand in her moisturized, manicured one. She has purple nails.

"You like purple."

She's still looking me over. "You're careful. You made me promise, too."

"Like you said, I'm smart. I'm a scientist."

She looks at me for a minute, and I can see her hiding away pity underneath something else, something like the way Bette looked when she was buying me clothes.

She signs some paperwork for the police, and they let her take me. It's light out again, and I've lost all sense of time. She pulls her little purple car into the drive-thru at McDonald's, and I know it must be morning since they have the full breakfast menu up.

She orders me a big bag of everything. "It's a little bit of a drive, Miss Layla."

I must be eating fast, because she reminds me to drink my orange juice.

Between bites, I think about my remaining resources. "So did the cops give you back my phone?"

"No, I'm afraid not. It's being looked at for evidence so they can find your mama."

"Well, they're not gonna find her on there." I eat a sausage patty in three bites and fish for more in the bag. "When can I get it back?"

"I don't know, but I will surely ask them for you. What do you mean, they won't find her on there?"

"She's never called my phone. Or texted. I don't have a number for her, except her office."

She sips a little coffee. "I see."

We drive in silence for a while. I lick the last of the hash-brown grease off my fingers.

"That was really good. Thank you."

"You're welcome."

"So where is Andy?"

She waits a second, checking the rearview before answering me. "He's in another foster home."

"Is it far? Are there other kids there?"

"It's a little bit far from where you'll be, yes. But he's the only kid there for right now."

"Have you seen him?" I ask her.

"Yes. I'm Andy's social worker as well."

"How was he?"

She's quiet for a minute, her purple lips pursed as she makes a turn. "It was hard for him at first. He had to adjust to a lot of things. But he's getting used to it now. He was excited to get new clothes. And he always asks for you."

The hot octopus reaches into my chest and squeezes my heart. "Really? And he's okay? He sleeps at night? And they know he's allergic—"

"To strawberries. Actually, nobody knew that until I saw it on your Twitter. Thanks for telling us that."

I don't say anything.

We pull into a long driveway in front of a really old-looking house with square posts holding up the porch. A tall blonde woman who reminds me of Bette comes through the door.

I turn back to tell Doc I don't want to go in, but she's already out of the car.

How is it that when I'm scared I age backward?

I step out of the car and see Doc has my backpack, but it looks mostly empty.

"Layla, this is Mrs. Joel. Mrs. Joel, Layla Bailey."

She walks down the steps and holds a hand out to me. "Hello, Layla. It's nice to meet you. I only found out you were coming a short while ago, but I'm so glad you're here."

"We both are." While Mrs. Joel is still holding my hand, a guy that has to be her husband is coming down the porch steps. "I'm Bertrand Joel."

"Nice to meet you, Mr. Joel." I shake his hand, too. I feel like a talking bird in a zoo.

Doc hands me my backpack. "You remember your promise, right?"

The Joels are walking toward their door together, letting me say goodbye to someone I've just met but who feels like my best friend in the world.

"They're not real people, right? They came from the Foster Parent Catalog from last year, and we're going to film a commercial."

Doc laughs hard this time, throwing her head back. "I told you. Nicest people I know. So, your promise?"

I look back at the big house. How weird can it be?

"Yes. I'll keep my promise."

"Good, and I'll keep mine. Now, they're expecting you back at school tomorrow. Martha—Mrs. Joel—will have some clothes for you, and you can't miss any more days. We have to keep you on track to graduate."

"Okay, Doc. And tomorrow?"

"Tomorrow you will have dinner with your brother," she tells me, promising again.

We both nod. She pats me on the shoulder as if to say goodbye and gets into her purple car. I turn back toward the front door, where the Foster Parent Commercial is about to begin.

Mrs. Joel gives me the tour. I have my own room. It was made up for a little girl, but everything is so clean and nice. When she gets a look at how dirty I am, she ends the tour in the bathroom. The tub is as big and as nice as Bette's, and the bath mat is soft like a bed for a little dog.

"There are feminine-hygiene products in this drawer here, when you need them."

"Oh. Thank you."

She leaves the room for a minute and I strip off my gross socks, peeling them off my feet the way you peel a black banana to see if it's still edible.

"Oh, I forgot!" She's at the door with a stack of folded clothes and towels. "We had to guess at sizes, but this will do for today. I'll go to Target tonight and get you a couple of outfits, but at least you'll have something clean to change into. And there's a clean towel for you, as well." She sets the whole thing down very gently and turns to leave again.

"Oh. Um, sorry. What should I call you?"

She smiles. "Most of the little kids call me Mom."

Did all the skin just peel off my face? She follows up quick with another option.

"You can call me Martha, though. If you like."

"Thank you, Martha. I'm . . . pretty tired. Is it alright if I go lie down after I get cleaned up?"

"Sure, sure, of course!" She zips out the door and closes it behind her. It doesn't lock from the inside, but foster kids can't be picky.

I run the shower first, just to get the first layer of dirt and BO off me. After that, I lie down in the tub and fill it as full as I dare.

When I slip between the clean sheets on the bed, wearing my clean shirt and underwear, I'm completely out of it. Everything feels like heaven. It's so much better than the canvas awnings and the sharp reek of chlorine that it seems ridiculous that that was the last time I was comfortable.

I laugh a little bit, because nothing makes sense. I laugh harder, and I think about Martha telling me I can call her Mom. My throat closes up and there's really only a little tiny plastic playground slide between laughing and crying. I shush myself like I used to shush Andy, and I fall deeply, deeply asleep.

Martha wakes me up by knocking on the bedroom door, and I'm sitting up before I'm even awake. I don't realize where I am at first, and it takes a minute. She pokes her head in.

"Hey, Layla, you slept through the whole day. It's morning. Are you feeling up to school today?" She's smiling.

"Yeah. Yeah, let me get myself up."

She comes in gently, almost on tiptoes. She sets a bag down on the edge of the bed. "I went and got you a couple of things for school, like

I said I would. And there's new toothbrushes in the bathroom, in the drawer above where the pads are. Can you get down to breakfast in the next fifteen or so?"

"I can, yeah."

"Okay. Do you eat meat?"

"Yeah. Yeah, I do. Opportunistic omnivore."

She hesitates a second, and I wonder if she knows what I mean. "Okay. Make your bed before you come down."

"Um. Okay."

She's gone as gently as she came. I take the bag to the bathroom with me and fumble open a toothbrush. I've had toothbrushes off and on the last few years. I try to remember to make Andy brush, but I forget. Like deodorant, it's something I learned about late. My gums bleed, and I spit it into the sink.

I open the bag and pull out a pair of leggings and a dress to go over them. Underneath that, there's jeans and underwear and a couple of T-shirts.

At the bottom of the bag, there's a red zip-up hoodie with a really cool design of thin black lines across the front of it. It's fleecy and soft inside, and I rub the hood with my thumbs for a minute.

I brush my hair more than usual. My curls open up into blooms of big frizz, and I wet the brush to calm them back down. I towel it just a little and hope it'll dry looking decent.

I pull on the first new outfit and zip the hoodie over it.

So normal. My damp hair looks almost human, and my clothes look so nice. I could be anybody. I could be the kid who lives in this house. I could be normal. Remove a single organism from its biome and see if it can flourish elsewhere. Can *H. sapiens* thrive in captivity? Probably not. Ask people in prison. But we adapt. I am adapting.

I take the hoodie off and carry all my stuff back to the room.

I've never made a bed before in my life.

I'm looking at it, and it can't be that hard. I've seen beds that were made. Kristi's was always made when we got to her room after school. And I've seen them on TV, and in the movies. Sometimes there would be two people making a bed together while they talked something out. Is it usually a two-person job?

The sheet on the bottom seems fine. The sheet on top of that I slept under, so it's all scrunched down because I kick in my sleep, according to Andy. I pull it up so that it covers the pillows. Did it start off that way? I don't remember. Then there's a thin blanket I pull up on top of that, and a fluffy peach comforter that I smooth out over the whole thing. That's made, right? Maybe I'm supposed to fold the whole thing down.

I think about my old loft bed, the pattern of spaceships on the bare black mattress. We only had one pillow, so I gave it to Andy and slept on my arm.

It's made.

I leave the bag with the clothes in it on top of the peach-and-gold dresser, and I add the clothes out of my backpack and my hairbrush to it. Now my backpack is just school stuff again. It feels light.

I carry it and my hoodie downstairs. Martha and her husband are in the kitchen. He's reading his iPad at the table, and she's setting down plates. I flash back to Mom making pancakes and pretending to be normal, promising this time would be different.

"Do you like juice?" Martha is holding open the stainless-steel door of her huge refrigerator.

"Can I have coffee, please?"

She frowns, putting her face against the edge of the door. "You really shouldn't. You're not done growing yet."

"Here." Mr. Joel is standing up, heading her way. "I'll show you how we used to make coffee milk when I was back at Brown. It's really good, but it isn't really coffee."

He pours a little coffee into a big glass of milk and adds a bunch of sugar. "Try this."

It tastes like coffee for babies, or really good chocolate milk.

"Thank you, Mr. Joel. It's good."

He smiles. "Think you could call me Bert?"

"Bert."

Everybody is smiling. I think about the chimps smiling at Dr. Goodall, how she smiled back. How it looks like the same thing to both species, but really can't be.

"Layla, don't let breakfast get cold, now." Martha is sitting down, waving for us to join her.

We sit down, and I'm already aiming my fork at the bacon on my plate when Martha stops me.

"Layla, we usually say a short blessing before we eat. You don't have to do it with us, but if you'd just hold off for a second?"

"Oh, sure. Sure." I put my fork down and my hands in my lap.

Martha smiles at Bert with her eyes closed, and he says it fast. It's short and sweet and it mentions me and my "trials" and it sounds like a wish for a good day at school. I can handle that. They say "Amen" together, and Bert digs straight in. I do, too.

Once he's eaten a bit, Bert starts. "So, Brookhurst Junior High, huh?"

"Yes." These eggs are so fluffy and good and hot.

"Eighth grade?" Martha is drinking regular coffee. I sip my baby coffee again.

"Yeah, uh, yes. Eighth grade."

"And we hear that you get really good grades. That you want to study something in the sciences." Bert looks like this is the best news ever.

"Yeah, um, yes. I really like lab work." The bacon is good too, and there's a muffin instead of toast. I try to pay attention to the conversation, but it's hard.

"Did you know I'm a biologist?" Bert is leaning forward a little, trying to get my attention.

"No, I didn't know that. That's really cool. What do you study?"

He laughs a little bit. "Fruit flies. Most biologists study fruit flies, because they live and die so quick. And my fruit flies are going to cure male-pattern baldness. Maybe you'd like to see the lab sometime?"

I nod, eating the top off the muffin with butter melting on my tongue. Swallow. Speak.

"Yeah, I'd really like that. Thank you. What . . . what do you do, Martha?"

She's a slower eater than me by a lot. "I was an emergency-room nurse for ten years, but then I decided to focus on being a foster mom. But I studied science, too. You have to, in nursing school."

"That makes sense." My plate is clean, my coffee milk is gone. I don't know what happens next.

"So," Martha starts. "So, your teachers have been updated about your situation. They will get you your missed work and help you catch up. And the kids you were having trouble with have been talked to about their behavior, so I want you to let us or Dr. Jones know if anyone is bothering you. Okay?"

"Okay." I know there's more coming, I just have to wait for it.

"Your videos have been getting a lot of traffic. And I know you're going to hear a lot from people on Twitter and the rest of the internet about it, because everyone's got an opinion . . ." She trails off and looks at Bert.

"Look, Layla. You're a big girl, and nobody is going to stop you from using the internet. It's been good for you so far, and you're going to have to learn to deal with the kind of attention you've been getting. Just remember that nobody's opinions about you are as important as your opinions about you. If anyone threatens you or scares you, tell an adult. But try to let the rest of it roll off you. It doesn't really matter."

They're both looking at me, and I have no idea what I'm supposed to do. There is no way that this is actually how parents talk to their kids. This is like the worst episode of any family TV show, the one where they try to teach you something. Here we are having breakfast in the kitchen as a family. Is this real life? Who am I supposed to be here?

"I'll keep that in mind. Thank you." I look down at my empty plate. When I look up again, they seem pleased. I guess that was good enough.

"If you're finished, go ahead and put your dishes in the sink. We should get ready to go here soon."

I do as I'm told. I run a little water over the dishes, like Bette always asked us to. I pull the hoodie on again and zip it up, pulling the cuffs over my hands.

"Do you like it?" Martha is carrying her own dishes to the sink.

"Yeah, I do. Thank you. Do you have to buy new clothes for every kid who comes here?"

She sets them down and pulls her own jacket off the back of her chair. "We get a little money for every kid who comes here, so that we can get them what they need. Some kids come with a suitcase, and others are like you and don't come with much of anything. But I saw that and thought it would look good on you. It really does."

"I really do like it. It's super warm. Thank you, again."

She smiles funny, looking at Bert again. It's like they can hear each other's thoughts and I'm just slightly too simple to get it. I pull my backpack on.

"I'll drop you at school, okay?"

She and Bert kiss on the cheek and say goodbye. Martha's car is as nice as Bette's. Bert pulls out of the driveway behind us in a smaller black car.

The drive to school lets me know where we are. It's the nice side of town, a mile or two from where Kristi lives. I could find my way back if I had to walk. When we pull into the drop-off loop, Martha hands me a phone.

"I know this is old, but it's really just for emergencies. It isn't worth anything, if it's stolen or sold. It will only call and text me or Bert or Dr. Jones. Or dial 911. It doesn't have internet. I want you to hold on to it in case something happens. And I'll be right here to pick you up as soon as school ends. Okay?"

I take it and hold it in my palm. It's nicer than my phone was. And I would have never thought of stealing it or selling it if she hadn't said that.

"Okay."

She looks at me for a moment, and I don't know if I'm supposed to say something else. Nothing comes to me, and I open the door and slide out.

Both hands deep in my hoodie pockets, I head to Raleigh's classroom.

The first day at a new school is so tense. I've been to a lot of new schools, so I know this feeling. People look at you way more than they talk to you. They definitely talk *about* you, and they think you can't tell. You sit wrong, you line up for lunch wrong, you eat with nobody.

I've been in the same district since fifth grade, which I think is a record. We've moved four times, but always in the same area. So I haven't had this feeling in almost four years.

But today, I have the first-day feeling times a million.

People are staring at me like I'm juggling live crabs (*Gecarcoidea natalis*, maybe) while I walk. They're also staying about as far away from me as you would from a person handling snapping, spidery red crabs.

First days mean no assigned seat, so at least I've got that. At least I don't have to listen to a teacher mispronounce my name, or stand up and introduce myself to the class.

The next time I have to do that I swear to god I will tell them that my name is Tardigrada, and I'm from the cannibal planet Cambria.

I sit in my assigned seat. Raleigh says my name during roll with such a careful casualness that I could throw my chair at him. Every head turns to hear me say "Present," as if I was going to announce the winning lottery number.

Today is never going to end.

Raleigh launches into the taxonomy lecture and I'm relieved to figure out that I'm not behind. I could pass the next test even if he gave it right now. Not so bad. I check out a bit after that, dreaming up a different life.

I snap in again when I realize everyone is back to staring at me.

". . . since the biome video contest was canceled, I've changed the rubric so that your videos will count as one-third of your midterm grade. Most of you did very well, so that should raise some scores. For those of you who worked in groups . . ."

It sounds like every phone in the room is buzzing. They must be tweeting about it. I guess the project was canceled because of me? At least now people are looking at their phones instead of at me.

I pull Martha's little black phone out of my pocket and try for a second to look at Twitter. Oh, right. It's blocked.

I can get on a computer at lunch.

Jane snorts somewhere in the back of the room. I didn't see her when I walked in, or Mackenzie. I know Kristi is in here somewhere. I am an expert in looking and not seeing. Normal. I am so normal. I have no reason to stare at anyone. They're all weirdos, not me. Just look at my clothes. So normal.

The bell rings and I don't move. I let people flow around me while I stare at my desk. Someone scratched a picture of an eyeball into it, maybe years and years ago. But it feels like it's just for me.

I walk up to Raleigh's desk. He's smiling at his crotch again, so really nothing has changed.

"Hey, I'm supposed to check in with you to see what I need to do to catch up."

He looks up at me and there's just a second when he looks terrified. It passes, but it's hard to forget.

"Layla. I loved your biome video. I watched it like ten times; I showed it to a lot of people. I was really impressed by your use of Latin taxonomy."

"Thank you?"

"Please believe me when I tell you I had no idea. None of your teachers did. We suspected there was trouble, but . . ."

"It's fine. I'm fine. It's nothing."

He's quiet for a minute. He looks like he's deciding something.

"So, do I have makeup work? Or?"

"How did you turn in your homework last week?" He's looking down again.

"I brought it to the office in the morning, before anyone was here."

He gives me this funny smile, like he's trying to hide that he's hurt. I know that face.

"You're caught up. You're fine. Keep up your attendance, and you're going to be just fine."

"Okay. Thank you."

I'm almost out the door when he calls out after me.

"That was really brave, Layla. That video. Like the bravest thing I've ever seen."

I don't say anything.

If it wasn't against school policy, I'd have my hood up during passing period. I wish I could be here but invisible. Like a ghost. Or inside a big tinted-glass ball.

I'm so sick of being stared at.

Someone says my name as I walk past, and I pretend to be as deaf as *Sepia apama*—a cuttlefish in the dark of the ocean without any sound receptors whatsoever in my strange, flashing body. I'm not even here.

I'm not walking into Honors English. I'm not sitting against the far wall. I'm not seeing Kristi sitting up in the front corner, hunched over something with Emerson. I'm definitely not seeing Mackenzie Biros walking up to me. Not staring at her bright-blue ballet flats.

"Layla," Mackenzie doesn't say, in a low and soft voice.

Alright, fine.

"Yeah?"

"I . . . I just wanted to say I'm sorry. About the other night. And also about a lot of things. I've always just kinda followed Jane, but I don't really like doing it. You know?"

"Sure." Bright blue with crisscrossed little straps. Just like real ballet shoes.

"I edited and re-uploaded that video, and tagged it #FindLayla. It's got like a billion views."

"Cool."

"Layla?"

"What?"

"Jane is sorry, too. She just can't admit it."

"Okay."

"Really. She totally feels bad about calling the cops. Her dad told her she should trick you into meeting somewhere so they could pick you up. And she got assigned to some community-service stuff, to make up for it. I did, too. She's going to have to give you a written apology when she's done." She's looking at her slippers.

If I threw up on those shoes, would they be ruined forever? Can you wash those? What does community service do for me, or for anyone else Jane pulled this shit on? What is the point of that? Literally vomiting on them would be more like justice.

I sigh. "I thought you were tired of following Jane. Aren't you tired of apologizing for her, too?"

"I guess. I didn't get in as much trouble as Jane, but the school counselor suggested I apologize, too. That's for me, not for her. I shouldn't have just let it happen. I just wanted you to know." One blue ballet slipper creeps up on top of the other, like she's trying to climb up herself. Like *Phoenicopterus ruber*, the classic flamingo, but in blue.

Am I supposed to thank her? I look up and yup, everyone is staring. I pull up my hood. Fuck policy.

"Okay, Mack. I get it. Thanks or you're forgiven or whatever."

She looks like that wasn't what she wanted to hear.

I try again. "Look, I'm having a weird time. Thank you for apologizing. Okay? I get it. I understand that it's over. I just want to be left alone."

"Okay. Okay." She's headed back to where Jane is holding her phone in both hands, carefully not looking at either one of us.

The rest of the day goes like that. People are either staring or working so hard not to stare that they seem to be in pain. If one more teacher calls me "brave" I'm going to bravely swallow my own tongue.

My biome video finally leveled off somewhere around five million. My Twitter account is a mess; I have too many mentions to find anything.

Erica's article about me came out the same day as the parking-lot video. It's not as bad as I thought it would be, and she admits that I ran out on her when I realized she was talking about me with Jane. I RT it.

The news made an edited version of the parking-lot video stream so that all the curse words are beeped out. I can't watch the whole thing, but it has about a million views, too. There are a couple of websites that say they're taking donations for my college fund or a trust fund for when I turn eighteen, but I'm sure they're scams. Maybe I'll dig through my thousands of emails later and see if someone is trying to give me money.

All I can think about to stay calm is that I'll see Andy tonight. It feels like it's been forever, like maybe he'll be older or taller or look different to me.

I expected a lot more makeup work than I've got. Most of my teachers reassured me that I'm doing fine overall, and every single one of them told me not to miss any more days. I said I wouldn't, but I don't know if I'm in any position to make promises.

I'm not in charge of where I'm going to be. That's not a new feeling. Life with Mom was always lived on the edge of maybe waking up in the middle of the night to pack a bag and never come back. Or finding an eviction notice stapled to the door. It wasn't up to me then and it isn't up to me now. I don't know how long I'll be with the Joels, or if I'll get put into something more permanent like an orphanage or whatever and have to change districts.

Nobody is in charge of taking me to school, are they? If I'm close enough, I'll walk there. Or take the bus, but I can't lie to a driver every day at the same stop, at the same time. Eventually I'll have to pay.

Really the only time I was in charge was when I was on my own. And I couldn't go to school then, or they would have put me back in this in-between place where I can't be sure. I'm back to being a subject.

So I promised Raleigh I wouldn't miss any more days. And when I said that, I hoped it would be up to me.

Martha picks me up in the same spot where she dropped me off. I see her before she sees me. Her face is all anxious like she's trying to find something she thought she lost. I wave to her, and behind the glare of the glass, her face relaxes. I pull myself up into the passenger seat and buckle in.

"How was it being back?"

"It was okay," I tell her.

"Are you very behind?"

"I guess not." I don't want to explain everything over and over again. How could I be behind? I've been on it the whole time.

She's smiling. "Well that's good news. Are you in any extracurriculars?"

"What?" How would I do extracurriculars? With what money? With who to pick me up after dark? Who does she think she's talking to?

She glances over at me just for a moment. I'm looking straight ahead.

"Do you do any stuff after school? Like sports or clubs or anything?"

"No." Why bother to explain?

Her brows knit a little. "No, I guess that must have been hard. Well, maybe in high school you'll be able to get into some fun stuff."

"Maybe. Depends on where I'll be."

She's quiet for a while. We get through the traffic around the school, and everything seems to go faster.

"So, we're going to see your brother tonight. Dr. Jones confirmed with me about an hour ago."

"Good. Yeah, she said she would bring him. That's good."

"Are you excited to see him?"

"Yeah, of course," I tell her.

"Is he your only sibling?"

I think for a second. He's the only sibling I've ever known, but there's a lot that I don't know. I never considered it before, but really I could have half brothers or sisters and I'd never know it.

"Yeah."

She sighs. "Just the two of you against the world."

So far the world is winning.

Tuesday Night, Dinner

Martha tells me to wash my hands and face and put my backpack in the bedroom. For a second I look at her like she's crazy, but I think it's only because it feels so strange to be told what to do like this.

I wash up. In the room, I find the bed has been remade. I was supposed to fold the blankets down, kind of. I slide my hands into the layers, trying to figure out how she did it. Maybe she would show me, if I asked.

When I come downstairs, the Joels are both sitting in their living room. All of their furniture is big and soft and colorful. It's the kind of thing people get when they have a bunch of kids who like to tear the place up. I guess they do have a bunch of kids, just not all at once.

Martha and Bert look really uncomfortable. I sit down in a chair across from the couch they're sharing, and I wait for it.

"So, we didn't think this was going to happen so soon," Bert says. "But you're going to be moving on tomorrow."

I don't say anything.

"We thought we could keep you for the week," Martha says. "Just to get you back into the swing of school and all. But Dr. Jones says some changes have to be made right now, because of your mother."

"What about her?"

They look quickly at one another. "We can't talk to you about that just now," Bert says. "Dr. Jones will be able to explain some of it. We just wanted you to hear it from us, so you could get used to the idea."

Martha is looking at the floor. She looks sick.

I have about ten seconds to think about this before the doorbell rings.

I don't wait. I'm done waiting. I run for the door and open it up and there's Andy.

He's wearing a little plaid shirt and khaki pants. His face is clean, and he looks like he's been fed and bathed every day. He flings himself at me hard, hugging me around my waist.

"Layla Layla Layla!"

I hug him back. "Hey, Andy! Hey. Hey, how are you?" The blue-ringed octopus is back, tentacles jammed in my ribs, beak stabbed in my throat.

"I been really good! I got new clothes! See?"

"Yeah, I see! I got some, too." I stand back to look at him. "Are the people taking care of you nice? Are they—"

"They're the *best*!" His eyes are bright and his vampire grin is wide. "They said I can call them Mom and Pop, and they make me breakfast every day, and I get stories at night, just like you tell! They know the one about the three gilly boats, too."

I laugh a little, just because he's so happy. "Yeah, you love the gilly boats. Are you doing your word lists? Do they help you with reading?"

"Mm-hmm. Look!" He's pulling off his blue backpack to show me his reading book from school. It's not the one I remember.

"Look look look. 'This is my hat. It is a red hat. It will not fit on the cat. My cat is a white cat.'" He smiles up at me, the happiest little vampire in the world.

"Really good!" I can't help but smile back.

He stuffs the book back in the bag; I can hear paper crumpling underneath it. Dr. Jones purses her lips at him and I remember that we're not alone.

"Oh, um. Mr. and Mrs. Joel, this is my little brother, Andy Bailey."

He waves at them, but takes a little step to be behind me. They wave back.

We sit in the living room and Andy sits on the floor in front of me. Dr. Jones pulls out her tablet.

"Layla, Martha told you that you're going to be relocated?"

"Yeah, that's fine. I'm ready to go whenever." In my head, I've already packed my bag. "Oh, here." I pull the little black phone out of my pocket and toss it onto the couch beside the Joels. "Thank you for letting me use that."

Martha looks down at it, still seeming like she's somewhere else.

Dr. Jones waits a moment before starting again. "You're going to be placed in a group home, like I told you that older kids usually live in? You'll be with a couple of other girls around your age, and you'll have contact with Andy. Also, you'll spend a little time talking to a doctor."

"A doctor like you?" Andy has one hand on top of my foot. She said "contact." She did not say "visits."

"Well, I have a doctorate in social work. I do some counseling, but you'll be talking with Dr. Eileen Yu, and she has a doctorate in psychology."

"Oh. I'm not . . . I don't need to talk to a—"

Dr. Jones stops me. "Nobody is saying that you're ill, or that you're dangerous, Layla. This is someone you can talk to about all the changes that have happened. She'll help you sort it all out and feel like you understand things better. Does that make sense?"

"I guess so." My face is hot. I put my hand on Andy's head.

Dr. Jones is looking at him now. "Andy, can you tell Layla about when you went and talked to Dr. Greenbaum?"

"Dr. G! He played Connect Four with me for a lot of games! And I won!"

Dr. Jones is nodding and smiling like it's show-and-tell day at the kindergarten. I don't want her to talk to Andy like she knows him better than I do.

"And do you guys talk sometimes?"

"Yeah, he told me it's okay if I miss Mom, and if I want to punch a pillow sometimes. And he told me a joke about big-mouth frogs."

If he was a puppy, they'd give him a treat. All the adults look so pleased.

At dinner, Andy sits next to me and eats carefully, with a knife and fork. Someone must have taught that to him, because I've never been able to stop him from eating with his fingers. He excuses himself when he burps. Even his lisp seems better.

Who is this kid?

After a little ice cream, his foster parents come and get him. He runs and hugs them exactly like he did to me. I'm so glad that he's okay and that they're taking care of him, but I also hate this so much I could burn down this house and dance in its tasteful ashes.

They did steal him after all, when they took him away. It'll never be the two of us against the world again, no matter what happens. It's all playing out the way I said it would. He'll forget the before-time and become somebody's kid. I'll always remember, and turn eighteen in some group home for gorillas who know sign language.

Andy turns around from hugging them and comes back to hug me. "I love you, Layla. I'm going to see you every week! And write you letters! Like this!"

Out of his pocket, he pulls a wadded-up piece of paper. It's the letter I wrote him and gave to Officer Benson.

"You got it!"

"Yeah! A policeman in a police car brung it."

"Brought it."

"Brought it to me. He said it was from my sister and asked me a bunch of times where you was. But I didn't know. And then Pop read it to me and I was so happy!"

I hug him again and look back to Dr. Jones. "I'm gonna walk them out."

She nods and looks back at her tablet. The Joels look at each other.

Andy's foster parents are already standing at the car, waiting for us. From the porch, I hold up one finger. *Just a second.*

I just want to see my brother for a minute more, just to see if we're still the same as we were.

He looks around like he's about to shoplift for the first time.

"Layla, I saw Mom."

"What? You saw Mom where? When?"

He looks over his shoulder again and whispers in his lispy, loud way. "I saw Mom the day after I got tooken away. I was sitting in a car, waiting for Dr. Jones to take me somewhere. I looked out the window and she was just standing there."

"Are you sure?" I'm staring at him hard. This kid is a terrible liar. He'd swear up and down he didn't eat any strawberries while his face was smeared with their sticky red guts and he was already swollen like *Colomesus asellus*, the Amazon puffer fish. I can see right through him.

He isn't lying.

"It was Mom! I know what Mom looks like."

"What did she say?"

"She didn't say nothing. The car was locked and I was in a car seat like a baby, so I couldn't get out. So I smacked on the glass and yelled at her to come get me."

He starts to cry. I put my hand on his shoulder, but I need him to finish.

"Did she try to get you? Did she say anything?"

He shakes his head, his breath catching on every word. "No. No. She didn't. Say. Nothing. She. Wouldn't. Get. Me." He takes a deep breath. "She just went like this."

He points to his chest. Then he hugs himself a little with both arms, then points to me.

"'I love you'? She said she loves you? I mean, she signed it?"

He shrugs, wiping his nose with his sleeve. "I guess so. She looked so sad. Then she looked scared and runned away. That was all."

That was all. That's Mom. That's life.

"I think Mommy does love me." He looks over his shoulder again. His foster parents look a little less patient than before.

I don't say anything.

He hugs me again. "I love you, Layla. I can say it with words. I know how."

"Me too, Andy. I love you, too. And I'll see you again soon, okay?"

He nods, wiping his face and shouldering his backpack. "Mom and Pop are nice. Come and visit them, okay? We got goldfish. And a big TV. And the lights are on every day."

I laugh a little and wipe my eyes. "Okay."

I watch them buckle him into a car seat, like a baby. I wonder how long it will be before they move him into some other place, too.

Back in the living room, conversation stops as soon as I walk into the room. I know from experience that this means nothing good.

"Layla, please sit down."

I sit back in the chair. The Joels stand up like they're one person.

"We're going to let you have some time alone with Dr. Jones." Martha's eyes are red like she's been crying, or like she's going to. Bert is looking at her, not at me.

"Okay. Good night."

"Good night," Bert says. And they're gone.

Dr. Jones and I are facing each other in two big chairs. I like her less right now than I used to. She's holding her tablet on her lap and using both hands to fix her headwrap, where it's loose in the back.

"Layla, I'm going to have to tell you some hard things. You might feel bad about this news, but you will be okay even after you hear it. Can you do this with me?"

My skin pricks all over. Nothing good.

I nod.

"The first thing I need to tell you is that Andy is not your brother."

"Bullshit." It comes out before I can even think. "Of course he's my brother. I remember when he was born. I took care of him since I was eight. He even looks like me."

Dr. Jones pulls up an eyebrow and stares me down. "Are you done?"

I don't say anything.

"Let me explain. Andy is your half brother. You two have the same mother, but two different fathers." From the leather case that holds her tablet, she pulls out some papers.

"Here is your birth certificate. Have you ever seen this before?"

I look it over. Female. Born December 21, 2005. In a state I didn't think I had ever been to. Mother: Darlene Grace Thompson. Father: Matthew Sean Bailey. Tiny footprints at the bottom.

Alright, so I was born.

"Here's Andy's, which I assume you've never seen."

Another sheet, from another state. It looks really different from mine. Male. Born May 18, 2014. Mother: Darlene Grace Thompson. Father: Daniel Brian Wendel. No footprints.

Andy's last name is Wendel. It always has been. I know the full Latin names of over a thousand creatures I've never seen, and I didn't know the correct taxonomy of my own brother.

"What the hell?"

I look up at Dr. Jones, who is watching me pretty carefully. "We think your mother registered you both in school with some faked paperwork to make you both Baileys. Maybe to keep you together, maybe to make it easier. I don't know."

I don't know. I don't know anything. Maybe nobody knows anything. I look over my own birth certificate again. I was born in Colorado. I've never been to Colorado.

"Mr. Wendel was very happy to hear from us. He had been trying to track down your mom and Andy for a long time. He saw your video and he knew that Andy was his son, but there wasn't enough information in it to find out where you guys were. But once we had Andy, we were able to reach out to him."

How long have I been holding my breath?

"Mr. Wendel—Andy's father—lives in Texas. He has two other boys and one girl in a big house with dogs. He wants Andy to go live with him."

I'm going to hold my breath until forever.

How long does it take to walk to Texas?

"Okay."

"Are you okay?"

"I'm fine."

I'm dying.

Dr. Jones looks at me for a long moment. "There's more coming, Miss Layla. Take some deep breaths."

The octopus stole all my deep breaths and took them down under the sea. Plus I'm dead, and I don't need to breathe anymore.

"We were able to track down your father from your records. You were right, he was in the military. He was never married and had no other children. He was killed in action in Afghanistan. In 2010."

What does it cost to lose something you never had?

No hot octopus. No more chair. No more soft, colorful living room. I am nobody, floating nowhere.

"Layla, breathe, honey. Deep breaths. Look at me. Say something."

I let out my breath and it rattles a little. "Okay. Okay. Okay."

I hold it again.

Dr. Jones reaches out and squeezes my hand a little. "I think we should continue this tomorrow. I think this has been hard enough."

I pull my hand back. "No."

She's holding her tablet flat between her palms. She's looking at me speculatively.

"Whatever the last thing is, just let me have it. Just give it to me so that I can get over it. Just let this be done."

She sighs and opens her tablet back up. "After I tell you, it won't be done. You'll just have to keep living it, that's the part I'm worried about. There is no being done. You understand?"

I understand.

Andy is gone from the driveway, but I stare at the spot where he used to be, buckled into a car seat, smiling. His vampire grin. My half brother. Half here and half gone. Half me and half strangers. Half mom and half some guy in Texas. What the fuck?

"Layla? Did you hear me?"

I turn back toward Dr. Jones. "No. Sorry, I zoned out."

She takes a deep breath and lets it out hard. "Your mother, Layla. Your mother—Darlene. She's gone."

"I know she's gone. I keep telling you all I have no idea where—"

"No. She's gone. She passed away. Three days ago, in a facility in Los Angeles. She overdosed on some medication and she died, Layla. Do you understand?"

I understand. All living organisms die.

I don't say anything.

"Layla?"

"What does it cost to lose something I never had?"

"What?"

I stand up and start running, not knowing where I'm going. I end up at the kitchen sink, throwing up on the ice-cream bowls that wouldn't fit in the dishwasher.

There is no being done.

The group home is close enough that I got to keep going to Brookhurst.

I turned fifteen the day after I found out I was an orphan for real. No more pretending. Like Dr. Goodall in the jungle, like a newly hatched baby *Chelonia mydas*, the sea turtle, I was on my own.

The day after that was the last day before winter break.

My midterm grades came back. I still have my 4.0. I put a copy on my website, FindLayla.com. I still might get adopted. Dr. Jones said it's hard because I'm older, and because Andy's record includes a violent incident from me. From when I broke his tooth. He told the truth about that. That means there's a violent incident on my record, as a foster kid. That changes things, no matter how good my grades are. That and the arrest don't look great. That's life.

Dr. Jones showed me the results of our DNA tests just before Christmas. The readouts look like scattered bars lined up in rows. She explained a little of how the machine works that does it. I want to see one in the lab, see how it takes our spit and tells us who we are.

Andy Wendel is my half brother. Daniel Wendel is his father; it says so right here in these bars.

My father's parents are also deceased. He has a sister somewhere, but nobody can find her. So my DNA just shows that I have the same mom as Andy. Dr. Jones says we have "common alleles."

He has different hair from me. Different skin, different eyes. I never thought about it. He's my brother.

My other doctor, Dr. Yu, always asks me how things make me feel. How do I feel knowing that my brother is not exactly as close to me on the taxa as I thought he was? How do I feel when I think about Mom? How do I feel about myself?

I tell her the truth. I feel the same as I always did. Like it's just me and Andy against the world.

Andy said he wanted to spend Christmas with me, but I said no. He'll have a better time meeting his dad and his new family, and I'm sure they're going to have presents and everything for him. He should go start getting used to them as soon as possible.

I wrapped up a book for him out of my backpack. It's the first Harry Potter book, and I've read it so many times I can almost recite it. He's not old enough for it yet, but he's reading so much better. It'll be time for books like that soon.

Dr. Jones brought me something for Christmas, but she said to put it in my footlocker or the other girls would get into it. It's a little plastic pack filled with small bottles of special shampoo and conditioner and some oily stuff for my hair. Strapped to the side of it there's a big wooden comb with teeth that sit far apart from each other.

While I was looking at it, she told me that my hair is hard to take care of because it's different. She said that this is a perfect time to get to know it, since I'm getting to know myself again as someone new. She told me there are girls on YouTube who have hair just like mine, and I can watch their videos and see what they do.

I'm back to where I started. Sitting in the bathtub with tools that I think will work, picking through my hair, trying to do better.

I had no father then, and I still don't.

I had no mother then, not really. And I don't now.

I had no brother then. He hadn't been born yet, and I didn't know he was gonna become my life and then slip out of it.

I make a video every week now. I talk about my house. About the bathtub. About the mushrooms and the mold and how any kid out there growing up like me isn't alone. The videos have started making money, and that's been really good.

Some things I don't talk about, like Mom or Dr. Yu. But thousands of people watch anyway. They listen to me talk, and sometimes they write and tell me their stories. Sometimes they're like me and sometimes they're not. Mackenzie Biros subscribes, and just leaves me hearts as comments. I don't know if Jane watches, and I don't really care.

Kristi and Emerson started a webcomic together. It's really funny and weird and deep. The three of us hang out sometimes, and it isn't awkward anymore. I can hug Bette without cussing her out in my head. Kristi stopped writing poetry. Amber Rodin started making hair-care videos.

Everybody wants to be internet famous.

Every once in a while, I go back and watch the biome video. I feel a lot older now; it's like watching video of myself years ago instead of a month. In a few days, I'll be able to say "last year."

That feels right. I feel older.

Andy's dad set him up on Skype to talk to me. He can video chat me whenever he wants, but I have to wait until it's my assigned computer time at the group home. Sometimes I talk to him at Kristi's on her MacBook. That's way better, and I don't have to be supervised. I am hoping to make enough YouTube money to buy a Mac of my own, but I can't have ads until I'm eighteen. That's life.

They let Andy's dad tell him about Mom. I told him, "You lost a mom and gained a dad. Overall, you're doing okay."

The last time we spoke, just before we said goodbye, he signed to me while he was talking.

"I." Points to himself.

"Love." The awkward bat-hug, arms crossed over his chest.

"You." He points at the screen in front of him, at his sister who is right there and so far away.

Nobody else knows that story. What we share is terrible, but it's ours and ours alone.

Like the world's most brilliant gorilla, I sign it back.

"I love you, too." I throw up two fingers at the end.

He grins, and his vampire smile is already gone.

When he winks out, the black screen reflects my own face back at me. I see Andy there, and just a little bit of Mom.

Just what we share.

That's life.

ABOUT THE AUTHOR

Photo © 2018 Debbie Reynolds

Meg Elison is a high school dropout and a graduate of UC Berkeley. Her debut novel, *The Book of the Unnamed Midwife*, won the 2014 Philip K. Dick Award. It was followed by *The Book of Etta* and *The Book of Flora* in Meg's Road to Nowhere trilogy. The author lives in the San Francisco Bay Area and writes like she's running out of time. For more information, visit www.megelison.com.